"These stories are swee~~~~~~~~~~~ Ireton achieves somethi~~~~~~~~~~~~~~~ ~~~~ ~~~~~ ~~~~~ tales: she reveals the true power and weight of kindness. If we have assumed that kindness is one of the minor virtues, somewhere far down a list headed by love, joy, and peace, *A Yellow Wood and Other Stories* will set us straight. I turned the final page with enormous gratitude for this reminder that a quiet life is not incompatible with a fruitful life."

—Christie Purifoy, author of *Placemaker* and *Garden Maker*

"There are so many wonderful layers to this story....Reading it was like being wrapped slowly and gently into a warm blanket surrounded by the arms of our heavenly Father."

—June Caedmon, author of *Pearl of Great Price* series

"Only K. C. Ireton could make a contemporary story sound like a classic. This was so lovely to read."

—Jody Lee Collins, author of *Mining the Bright Birds*

"In *A Yellow Wood and Other Stories*, K. C. Ireton offers stories of the kind I like best—stories that yield even more empathy and humanity upon a second and third reading, whose settings and characters make me want to pay a neighborly visit again and again. With the perceptive voice of O. Henry's narrators and the unhurried, beauty-loving eye of L. M. Montgomery, Ireton draws our attention to the power of small gestures of love and kindness, leaving them to sink in and take root long after we've closed the book. This collection is well worth befriending, and I recommend it with delight."

—Amy Baik Lee, author of *This Homeward Ache*

"I loved every word of K.C. Ireton's *A Yellow Wood and Other Stories*. The...deep layers of complexity and untold secrets ring true to real life—an undeniable testament to Ireton's talent as a storyteller."

—Maribeth Barber Albritton, author of *Operation Lionhearted*

"K.C. Ireton brings a particular quality of beauty to life in *A Yellow Wood and Other Stories*: the beauty of grace. Something in her finely crafted characters reminds me of Elizabeth Goudge, portraying a range of human qualities and predicaments, yet held in a certain cast of light. She restores my love of short fiction, and utterly captivates me with her title story, "A Yellow Wood." Just as when reading *Pilgrim's Inn*, I am elevated as I read Ireton's work, and that, too, is grace spilling out of pages into life. What a beautiful, gracious work this is!"

—Lancia E. Smith, Publisher & Executive Director, Cultivating Oaks Press, LLC.

# A Yellow Wood
## and other stories

K. C. Ireton

ML
Mason Lewis
Press

"Reflections" was originally published in *Cultivating*, July 2018, under the title "Reflections: Bringing the Outside In" ~ "Being Grace Kelly" was originally published in *Cultivating*, April 2018 ~ The final sonnet in "A Yellow Wood" was originally published under the title "October" in *Cultivating the Sacred Ordinary: A Poetry Collection*, edited by Leslie Anne Bustard and Amy Malskeit, © 2023 by The Cultivating Project. https://thecultivatingproject.com.

Cover image: Brandon Green on Unsplash
Cover design: PaperVale

ISBN: 978-0-9896725-4-2

Printed in the United States of America

For Sandy and Mary K.

# Contents

# A Yellow Wood

## 1

Maggie rinsed off the last of the breakfast dishes and placed them in the drying rack. "All right, Gram. I think I'm ready."

"To the attic we go, then." Gram grabbed a large cardboard box and handed it to Maggie. Inside the box were a dozen other flattened boxes along with a roll of black garbage bags and another of white garbage bags. She picked up another almost identical box and led the way up the stairs. At the top of the second flight, she paused at a white door whose paint was chipped and peeling and looked over her shoulder. "I don't know when this place was last cleaned. I don't think Helen came upstairs in this house for the last dozen years or so."

Maggie nodded. "I am prepared for the worst."

But she wasn't.

Tables, desks, chairs—some broken, some not—wooden chests, crates, boxes, and paper bags were stacked several feet high the whole length and width of the room; at one end of the attic the stacks reached almost to the gabled ceiling. Shelves on the low side walls were lined with old lamps—both electric and kerosene—vases, stacks of dishes, small boxes and bins overflowing with electrical cords, light bulbs, dried roses, socks and shoes, and dozens of old Mason jars full of buttons, marbles, keys, and rusty screws and nails, all of it coated with a thick film of dust. Maggie could see the dust motes dancing gleefully in the morning light that filtered through the torn curtains on the window at the far end of the room. "Oh Gram, where do we start?"

"We start by opening that window. Can you get to it?"

Maggie climbed around and over furniture and boxes to the far side of the attic, sending years of settled dust whirling into the air. She sneezed six times before she managed to get to the window. And then she had to clamber back for a hammer to get the window loosened from its frame so it would open.

"Good," Gram said. "A job begun is half done."

"But we haven't done anything yet."

"Yes, we have. We've opened the window."

Maggie almost laughed. Or maybe it was a sob. She couldn't really tell.

"Since you're back there," Gram instructed, "start with that stack of clothes beside you. I'll work from my end, and we'll meet in the middle."

"Next year, maybe."

Gram laughed. "You might be right, dear." She pulled a roll of white plastic garbage bags out of her cardboard box and tossed it to Maggie. "If it looks nice enough to give to the church for their jumble sale, put it in one of these." She tossed over a roll of black plastic bags. "If it's junk or broken beyond repair, use these. And if you want to keep it or if it looks like a family piece, set it aside. Once we clear a path through this mess, you can put the things we're keeping in one of these boxes. We'll take the full bags downstairs before lunch."

"And call it a day?"

"That was our deal." Gram smiled. "Now get to work."

Maggie pulled a dress off the pile of clothes that lay on top of a stack of boxes that lay on an upturned desk that lay on top of a large wooden chest. The dress had once been blue but now was gray with dust and eaten by moths. She shoved it in a black plastic bag. "By the look of this stuff, we'll have this whole roll of bags filled by noon." As she pulled off more dusty sweaters, shirts, and slacks—polyester, no less—she sneezed again, then grimaced and shook her head and wondered why on earth she had traded her final year of college to come sort through her great-grandmother's junk. But even as the thought came to her, she knew it was the other way around. She had come to sort through her great-grandmother's stuff so she wouldn't have to go back to college.

Three hours and a dozen bags later, Maggie had managed to clear enough floor space to set the desk upright on the floor under the window. "It's a nice view," she said. "And it's a beautiful desk."

She ran her hand over the weathered pine surface, bowed a little with age, and opened the small drawer in the desk's apron. It was empty, save for a dead blue bottle fly. Maggie slid the drawer shut. She stood for a moment, staring out the window at the hillside that sloped down to the valley with its crisscross lines of stone walls and the green fields between.

Turning away from the window, she lifted the lid of the wooden trunk on which the table had been sitting. It was locked. Maggie looked at it more closely. It looked old. Very old. Its edges were reinforced with metal straps, it had a metal handle on each end, and on the front, just below the lock, was the monogram EB. Maggie was curious. She felt around its sides for a key. She got down on her knees and looked on the floor nearby. No key. She sat back on her heels and looked around. Her eyes fell on the row of Mason jars, two of which were full of keys. She climbed over a table and two dressers, grabbed one of the jars of keys, and returned to the trunk. Looking at the lock, she knew most of the keys wouldn't work. She needed an old skeleton key. She dumped the jar of keys on the desk, spread them out, and discovered three skeleton keys. None of them worked. She returned the keys to the jar, clambered back over the table and dressers, putting that jar back and grabbing the other. This one held five skeleton keys. Maggie tried them one after another. When she slid the third one into the lock and turned it, the lock clicked open. She lifted the lid and gasped.

"Holy cow, Gram. Look at this!"

"Maggie, dear, I couldn't get back there without a crane."

"Books, Gram. Old ones. They're beautiful." She lifted out a red leather volume and looked at its spine. Shakespeare. Carefully she opened it. The endpapers looked like an aerial view of ocean waves. Even more carefully she turned the page. It was blank except for the initials EB written in beautiful script in the upper right corner. Maggie wondered briefly who EB was before she turned the page. Opposite the title page was a painting, or maybe it was an engraving, of a statue—a man in 18th century garb sitting on a stone, with two women dancing beside him. The printing beneath the picture was faded and blurred.

She raised the book closer to her face to try to read the words, and the wonderful smell of old books filled her nostrils, for a moment overpowering the dust in the air. She closed her eyes for a moment and breathed it in. When she opened her eyes, she tried to make out the words beneath the picture but it was hopeless. She had no idea who the sculpture was supposed to represent. Shakespeare with his muses? She gently ran her hand over the title page, which was surprisingly soft and smooth beneath her fingers, and read: "The Dramatic Works of William Shakespeare Revised by George Steevens. Vol. 1." She wondered who George Steevens was and why his last name had three e's. At the bottom of the page were the Roman numerals MDCCCII. It took her a moment to decipher them.

"Gram!" she exclaimed. "This book was published in 1802!" Shoving the keys back into the jar, she set the book gently down on the desk, and picked another out of the trunk. Shakespeare. And clearly part of the same set. She placed it on the desk on top of the first book, and pulled out another. Altogether there were nine volumes of Shakespeare. Then three volumes of Spencer's *Faerie Queene*. Two volumes of Boswell's *Life of Johnson*. Johnson's *London* and *The Vanity of Human Wishes*. Almost two dozen volumes of Sir Walter Scott. *Lyrical Ballads*. Four of Jane Austen's novels, each in three volumes.

Maggie shook her head, wondering and delighted and scarcely able to believe what she was seeing. "Gram!" She held two of the Austen books up so Gram could see. "Look at these! They're gorgeous!"

Gram looked up and smiled. "Finder's keepers, dear."

Maggie's eyes went wide. "Really?"

"Helen left it all to your grandpa, and he left it all to me, so it's mine to do with as I please." Maggie's grandfather had

13

died three years ago. "If you want them, they're yours. It's about lunchtime. You at a good stopping place?"

"No way. I want to see what else is in here."

"All right. I'll start lunch and holler at you when it's ready." Gram went downstairs, carting two bulging black bags with her, and Maggie stayed to look at the books. The entire desk top was covered with stacks of books by the time she pulled out the last one, a faded but still lovely little copy of *Paradise Lost*. She opened the cover. Inside lay a thin parcel of papers, folded into a square, yellow with age, and tied with a faded blue ribbon. Maggie set the book in her lap, carefully untied the ribbon and even more carefully unfolded the papers. There were three sheets of paper, and on each side of each paper in a beautiful flowing hand was a poem followed by the initials E.B., a month, and the year 1818. Maggie held the pages gently, a little awed that in her hands were poems penned 170 years ago. When she glanced at the poems, she recognized their square shape and quickly count- ed the lines. Fourteen. These were sonnets. She began to read the first one. By the time she had finished it, her chest felt hollowed out by the words and her hands were almost shaking.

"Maggie!" Gram called from downstairs. "Lunch!"

Maggie glanced at the papers again, then shakily re-folded them, tied them with the blue ribbon, and put them in the desk drawer. She would read them, all of them, later. She decided she wouldn't tell Gram about them. Not yet. Maybe not ever.

## 2

He cupped in perfect palms my girlish face
And said he loved me—loved me! I believed—
Surrendered all to him—my deepest place—
Of holies holiest—and he received
Or rather took, stole, gobbled greedily
Until a surfeit gorged his empty soul—
No sacrifice can sate so speedily
As flesh upon an altar, burnt to coal
Black as the emptiness behind his eyes
The day I knew myself unloved, deceived—
Grey day when he forswore my sacrifice
And offered me to other gods. Bereaved,
Bereft—my girlish face ashamed—I fled
His tabernacle, though my soul still bled.

—E.B., January 1818

❧

Maggie lay on her back on a flattish patch of grass on the west slope of the hill. To her right, in the distance, she could hear the occasional bleat of a sheep. On her face, she felt the dimming heat of the setting August sun. It would sink over the far hills soon, and she would be in shadow. Her hands resting on her still-flat belly, she stared up at the blue bowl of sky, fleecy clouds shifting shape, and shivered. The sonnet she had read that morning had almost undone her. She had not had the courage to return to the attic to read the others, though she knew she would, in time.

Something cold and wet touched her cheek, and she sat bolt upright in surprise and fear—only to find herself looking into the gentle, smiling face of a collie. She grinned back at the animal.

"Now, Floss," said a man's thickly accented voice, "I know it's not every day we find a lass lying on the hillside, but that's no cause for being so forward."

Maggie looked up at him, backlit by the sun; she could see only his silhouette. He extended a hand to help her up, but she ignored it and scrambled to her feet without his assistance.

"I'm sorry Floss startled you," the man said. His accent wasn't English. Welsh, perhaps? She took a few steps down the hill, to get the sun out of her eyes, and to see him more clearly. She didn't like looking into a person's face only to see a shadow.

The man extended his hand again. "James MacKinnon."

This time Maggie shook it. "Maggie Lowell."

"Ah!" James smiled, and Maggie realized he wasn't as old as she had at first thought, maybe thirty. "Lowell. You must be Helen's family then?"

"Yes. She was my great-grandmother." Maggie nodded and waved in the direction of the stone house whose roof was just visible over the crest of a hill to the northwest. "I'm staying with my grandmother for a few months. She inherited the house from Helen."

James nodded. "Kezzy told me she'd met you."

"Yes," Maggie said again. "She brought over some lettuce and beans and tomatoes yesterday. And an apple pie. It was very kind—and delicious. We ate the beans for dinner, the apple pie for breakfast, and the lettuce and tomato on sandwiches at lunch today."

"She'll be glad you enjoyed it. She always grows more food than we or the neighbors can eat. Most folks lock their doors when they see Kezzy coming with a basket of food." He grinned, which made him look still younger. "She sells some of it in town, but even so, there's always extra. She used to give it to Helen, but she never ate much, so I know she's glad to have new folks to foist it onto."

Maggie grinned back. "Well, please tell her that Gram and I are more than happy to have fresh produce foisted upon us anytime."

James laughed. "Be careful what you ask for or you'll find yourself drowning in zucchini." He began to move across the hill toward the sheep, and Maggie fell in step beside him.

"I like zucchini," she said stoutly. "I like most vegetables. And I never tasted any tomato as good as the one I had on my sandwich today."

"I'll tell Kezzy that. It'll make her happy. You can always come by and pick whatever you like. Stonewold is just over that rise," James said, pointing to the south. "She wouldn't mind your just harvesting for yourself."

"Really?" Maggie said. "That's awfully generous."

"She's a generous woman."

Maggie's curiosity got the better of her. "How are you related to her? Your aunt?"

James shook his head. "No relation, not by blood. But she and Bill have been good friends to me these past five years."

"Bill?"

"Her husband. You won't see him much. Keeps to himself.

17

The man's the definition of taciturn. But he's as generous as she is, in his way. He used to stop by to see Helen every day, load up her wood bin, do any odd job she couldn't manage. Days he couldn't come, he'd send Kezzy or me."

He grinned again. "Helen didn't like that much. Not at first anyway. She thought I was a daft fool, and Bill a dafter one for taking me in. I'd be bringing in her wood to stack on the hearth, and she'd be sitting in that big chair of hers, like the queen on her throne, wrapped in a quilt or a shawl. 'Put it over there,' she'd say, pointing imperiously with her spectacles. 'Not there, James MacKinnon, you great lummox. There!'" He laughed. "I took it for awhile, but one day, I turned to her and said, 'Helen, you're as tart as a lemon, and I've had enough lemon today. So if you'd like to stack your own wood, be my guest.'

"She didn't miss a beat, just laughed right out loud and said, 'Today's the day I finally like you, James MacKinnon. I've been waiting nearly a year for you to say something ornery to me. I do believe there might be Scottish blood in your veins after all.' And she hauled herself out of that chair, took me by the shoulders, and nipped me on the chin." He grinned at the memory.

Not Welsh, Maggie thought. Scottish. She wondered how he'd ended up here in the border country. She didn't ask. Instead she said, "I wish I'd known her. I only met her once. She came to Spokane—that's in Washington State, where I grew up—when I was six. I barely remember what she looked like." Then she grinned. "I do remember that I was a little bit afraid of her. I guess she must have been sharp-tongued then, too."

"No doubt. People are like sheep. They—"

"Maggie!" A voice called from the far side of the hill, wavering in the distance.

"That's my Gram," Maggie said.

18

"Maggie!" The voice called again. "Maggie, where are you?"

"I'm here, Gram!" Maggie called back.

But apparently Gram did not hear, for a moment later, she called again, a note of anxiety in her voice. "Maggie!"

"She sounds worried." Maggie grinned. "Probably afraid I'll be trampled by one of your sheep."

"Maggie!" The anxious tone had increased.

"I'd better go," Maggie said. "It was nice to meet you."

"Likewise." James touched the brim of his hat, a gesture Maggie found both amusing and appealing.

Gram appeared at the top of the hill.

Maggie waved at her.

"Mary Magdalen Lowell!" Gram called to her in exasperation, waving for her to come.

"Oh dear. I'm in for it now," Maggie muttered.

James gave her a quizzical smile and raised his eyebrows in a question.

Maggie was tired of answering that question, so she pretended not to understand. "She only uses my full name when she's upset."

James nodded, but the quizzical smile remained. "Mary Magdalen?" He pronounced it *Maudlin*, the way Gram did.

Maggie said, "Maggie's short for Magdalen," and then, as if this explained everything, "My mom's a New Testament scholar, and my dad's a biblical theologian."

James nodded, but she could still see the question in his eyes and the smile on his lips, as if he thought it were funny. It was the laughing question in almost everyone's eyes when they learned her full name. Especially men's. Not for the first time, she resented her professor parents' making her name a teaching moment for everyone who met her.

"Magdalen?" James said again. "Like the—" He broke off abruptly and looked away.

But Maggie knew the next word, even though he hadn't said it. "No," she said icily and gave him a withering look. She turned on her heel, and stalked up the hill toward Gram, angry at the world, at men in general, and at James MacKinnon in particular. *What is wrong with you? It's not like that's the first time some ignorant yokel has asked that question.* But she knew exactly what was wrong. For the first time in her life, that question hit too close to home. *At least prostitutes get paid for sex. I did it for free.* Tears sprang to her eyes. She wiped them fiercely away with the back of her hand. *The more fool me.*

## 3

"They wandered in the wilderness of Sin."
Sin is a place to worship golden calves—
My calf, a man; my wilderness, within.
Town's fetid fogs—their muck and moil—mere halves
The sand and ash and soot that smirch my soul's
Depths—depths I gave to him—that he received
And filled and then reviled and ripped—great holes
To seep such swirling mad cloud-thoughts. Conceived
I ne'er till now such fearsome demon-dust
Could fog my heart, my head, leave me alone
Though compassed round by merry friends—they jest
And laugh—I curve my lips but inward moan.
It's said life grows in deserts—seed and tree;
A fearful, fearful truth—it grows in me.

—E.B., February 1818

❦

Two days later Maggie sat with her back against the sun-warmed stones of one of the ubiquitous stone walls that crisscrossed the hills and valleys of Herefordshire. The checkerboard of rock walls, green pastures dotted with sheep or cattle, and golden fields unfolded before her almost to the river. The Land of Counterpane, she called it, remembering her mother snuggling her down under her own quilt and reciting the Stevenson poem to her. She said it softly to herself now.

> *"When I was sick and lay abed,*
> *I had two pillows at my head,*
> *And all my toys beside me lay*
> *To keep me happy all the day."*

She wondered who E.B. was.

> *"And sometimes sent my ships in fleets*
> *All up and down among the sheets;*
> *Or brought my trees and houses out*
> *And planted cities all about."*

"Gram," she'd said over her tomato sandwich at lunch, "some of those books I found the other day were labeled E.B." She'd taken the sonnets from the desk drawer yesterday and read them. She wasn't about to tell Gram about them, but she was curious about their author. "Do you know who that might be?"

"No idea, dear," Gram had said. "But there's a family Bible around here somewhere. When we unearth it, we can look at the family tree and see if there's an E.B. in our past."

Maggie sat up straighter, leaning away from the stones at her back. She could almost see Stevenson's poem play out before her and raised her voice a little, the way her mother used to, rising to a crescendo in the last stanza.

> *"And sometimes for an hour or so*
> *I watched my leaden soldiers go,*
> *With different uniforms and drills,*
> *Among the bed-clothes, through the hills."*

A swift motion caught the edge of her vision. She turned her head to see James leap the wall and drop onto the ground beside her.

She jumped a little. "You startled me!"

*"I was the giant great and still,"* he said,
*"That sits upon the pillow-hill*
*And sees before him dale and plain,*
*The pleasant land of counterpane."*

"Showing off?" she asked, and hated the waspish sound of her voice.

He gave her a sheepish grin. "A little. Stevenson was Scottish, you know."

Maggie did know. But she did not know what to say. She turned her face away from him, toward the valley.

He swept his arm before him. "I sometimes think of that poem, too, when I see these fields. My dad used to read Stevenson to me when I was a boy."

Maggie still said nothing. She stared out at the valley and felt her cheeks burn with shame over her behavior to him the other day. She could have been more gracious. *And he could have kept his question to himself and his mouth shut.*

James cleared his throat. "I'm sorry I snuck up on you. I was afraid if you saw me coming you'd walk away."

She almost looked at him then. "Is that your way of apologizing for being a total jerk?" The words were out before she'd even thought about them, and she could have bitten off her tongue. So much for gracious.

"Well, no, it wasn't, though I do think I owe you an apology."

Maggie's shame evaporated, replaced by irritation. "You

*think* you owe me an apology?" She could scarcely conceal the scorn in her voice.

James nodded, seeming either to not notice or not mind her tone. "I clearly upset you the other day, and you're clearly still upset. But I confess I'm not sure what I said or did that makes me" —he paused—"a total jerk."

"Are you serious?" Maggie gave him a contemptuous look.

"I'm sorry." James shook his head. "I hate to be so thick. It has to do with your name, I think. Magdalen." He hesitated a moment. "Like the college at Oxford."

Maggie stared at him a moment, then looked back out at the valley, her scorn sucked out of her and shame rushing back in a torrent that set her cheeks burning hotter than before. Is that what he had been going to say? Like the college at Oxford? And she'd bitten his head off. She felt horrified as well as ashamed. She had no idea what to say and couldn't seem to find her voice anyway. She swallowed and shook her head. "No," she finally said. "I mean, yes, like the college, but no, you don't owe me an apology." She took a deep breath and slowly exhaled it. "It seems I owe you one." She glanced at him, and quickly back out at the valley. "I—I misunderstood you. I'm sorry."

James was silent a moment, and she could feel his eyes on her face. She kept her own eyes steadily on the valley, though she saw none of it, her attention absorbed by the embarrassment she felt. She also felt she owed him an explanation. "Most people think that Mary Magdalen was a prostitute. She wasn't—she was actually one of Jesus of Nazareth's most faithful followers. For her faithfulness, she was one of the first to see him resurrected. In fact, she's the only person mentioned as a first witness to the resurrection in all four Gospels. But most people don't know that. They just think of her as a prostitute, even though

24

there's no evidence of that. And men tend to find it funny that my parents would name me, as they think, after a prostitute. It gets old."

"They *say* this to you?"

"Oh, yeah. It happens a lot."

"Gits."

Maggie grinned. "Yes."

"No wonder you thought I was a prat."

"I'm sorry." Maggie kept her eyes on the valley below and hoped James wouldn't ask any more questions.

She felt the moment when he looked away from her and out over the valley. "The Land of Counterpane," he said. "Rather pleasant, isn't it?"

Maggie nodded, relief flooding her. "Yes. It's—peaceful somehow. It looks ordered and—and right, as if everything were where it belonged."

"So it is," James said. He pointed to a field off to their left. "That's the border fence of Stonewold. All this land here belonged to Helen. She let it to us, though, so Bill and I frequently graze the sheep all the way to that boundary there." He pointed down the hill and away to the right, but Maggie wasn't sure which boundary he meant; the land was crisscrossed with stone walls. He continued to talk quietly, naming the farms and the neighbors as he moved his hand across the Land of Counterpane. Maggie followed his pointing finger with her eyes, trying to listen, and asking the occasional question. She was deeply aware that he was being kind to her, and that she did not deserve it. His easy conversation told her that he had accepted her apology, that he would not ask awkward questions, and that he wanted her to feel welcome and at home here. By the time he was finished with his little geography lesson, she was beginning to.

"Thank you," she said, and smiled at him. "That was really helpful. How long have you lived here?"

"Five years."

"You seem to know the land like you've lived here always. I never knew anything, really, about the places I've lived. Just street names and where the stores are." Even as she said it, she suddenly realized it was true. And shallow. Her knowledge of the places she lived was about as deep as the sidewalk or the asphalt.

"Not a lot of streets around here," James said. "Just roads and lanes. And no stores. Just fields."

Maggie gazed out over the Land of Counterpane. "I suppose that's why it's so peaceful," she said. They sat in silence for several moments, and Maggie realized that James had the gift of self-effacement. His presence was not awkward. He was as peaceful as the land itself, quietly fading into the background when one's focus was elsewhere. She turned her head and gave him a quiet smile. "Thanks for—for coming to find me. It's nice to have someone other than Gram to talk to. She's great—the best grandmother in the world—but I'm glad to know someone my own age."

James shook his head. "I don't think I'm your age."

She gave him an appraising glance, taking in his long lean frame, his deeply tanned face, the lines around his mouth that suggested he laughed easily and often, and the lines around his eyes that spoke plainly of suffering. Her smile faded and she looked abruptly away. "I don't think so, either," she said, forcing the smile back to her lips and trying to keep her voice light. "I'm 22."

"Thirty."

Maggie shrugged. "It's closer than 75."

James laughed, such a contagious shout of joy that she found herself laughing with him.

She realized it had been a long time since she'd laughed.

# 4

O God, bow down Thine ear and hear—O hear—
For Thou alone may save. My Castle, Crag,
Defense, O draw me out the net—this fear
That stalks my soul and doth my body drag
Down heavy, pulled like tides by moon to drown
In darkness of iniquity—consumed.
Reproached, avoided, burned by friends' cold frowns
And broken like a vessel ocean-doomed
I toss upon grey waves. No shore is near—
No one but Thou. Have mercy! Take my part—
O save my salt-soaked soul—'tis sere and seared
And Thou alone may slake my charrèd heart,
May tabernacle me on foreign sands
Wandering, afraid, alone—into Thy hands.
                                        —E.B., March 1818

❧

Maggie's days fell into a rhythm—mornings she spent with
Gram, sorting through Helen's belongings; after lunch Gram
rested or read, and Maggie went outdoors to walk through the
fields or sit and stare at the river or read E.B.'s sonnets. She kept
them with her always—E.B., whoever she was, seemed a kindred
soul. She had known shame and suffering—and though Maggie

28

did not quite feel she could consider herself to be suffering, she knew enough of shame and regret to find her current situation painful, at best.

Often on her jaunts she ran into James and walked with him, quoting Stevenson at him and learning the various landmarks they passed and how to tell a Leicester sheep from a Ryeland.

In early October the sun-warmed days turned misty and damp, but most afternoons Maggie simply donned her boots and jacket and tramped through the rain and mist, just to be out-of-doors and not breathing the dust that shrouded her great-grandmother's house. And then, after almost two weeks of mist and rain, came an afternoon of clear, pale blue sky. Weak autumn sunshine shone on the damp fields, turning their green to deepest emerald. The air was crisp and cool, with that tang of falling leaves and wet earth that always made Maggie feel both happy and sad at the same time. She put her hands in her jacket pockets as she walked, and touched the brittle paper of E.B.'s sonnets.

Leaning against the cold stone of a low wall bordering one of the many pastures, she looked down toward the river. Sheep grazed in the meadow on the other side of the wall, two different breeds. She smiled to think she knew that and wondered if she would run into James today.

After fingering the pages of the sonnets, she gingerly pulled them out of her pocket and held the folded pages in both hands. They felt holy to her somehow. She longed to know what had happened to E.B. Who was she? How had her poems ended up in Helen's attic? Maggie imagined many scenarios, but without more clues than the sonnets provided, she would never know—and she wanted to know. Her own future seemed to depend on

E.B.'s future, now in the past. Could she discover that past—but how if it were tragic? E.B. met kindness, Maggie knew, but did she know affection, or love? Had she been able to let go of the deep pain that her lover's betrayal and abandonment had caused her? Had she lived a happy life?

"You're awfully deep in thought." James's voice startled her out of her reverie.

Maggie started. "Must you keep doing that? Sneaking up on a person and frightening her half out of her wits?"

He stood on the other side of the stone wall and grinned at her. "I'm sorry. I tried to warn you. I cleared my throat twice, *and* I coughed."

Maggie's cheeks flushed, and she laughed apologetically. "It's okay. I was just—thinking."

"Aye." James's grin widened. "I gathered that." He gestured to the papers in her hand. "A letter from home?"

She shook her head. "I found these in a trunk in Helen's attic." She hadn't planned to tell anyone about the sonnets. She had not shown them to Gram. She had not even mentioned them. She could not bear to. Maggie felt protective of them, of E.B. herself. But when she glanced at James, his face was so kind, his eyes so attentive that she found herself continuing, "They're sonnets. Six of them. By a woman. No signature, just her initials and the year—1818. I've no idea who she was, or how her verses ended up in a trunk in Helen's attic. It's all rather mysterious."

"May I read them?"

Maggie hesitated. But how could she refuse now she had told him about them? It would be rude, and they were sonnets after all, and James was a shepherd; perhaps he would not entirely understand them; certainly he could not know how they affected her. All this flitted through her head in half a second, as he looked at her with his kind eyes and gentle smile, and she saw her arm extending and her hand surrendering the precious papers to him. He read them silently, his face inscrutable, then folded them carefully and handed them back to her, and still said nothing. He looked quietly out over the meadow and down to the river.

Maggie's heart pounded. How much had he understood? How much had he guessed? She wished she had kept her mouth shut and the sonnets to herself. What had possessed her to show them to him?

"I miss poetry," James said softly.

His words were so unexpected that Maggie blinked and gave herself a mental shake. "You—what?"

He smiled, though he still looked out at the fields. "I miss poetry. I've read or remembered more of it in the five weeks I've known you than in the past five years."

Maggie studied his profile, wondering.

"I studied literature at Oxford," he said, "for eight years."

Maggie's cheeks burned. Her arrogance and presumption! Only a shepherd! Thank God he could not read her thoughts. Couldn't understand a sonnet!

"By the time I was done with my D.Phil.," James continued, "I hated poetry. I hated literature. I almost hated words. I couldn't remember why I'd spent so many years studying them. We analyzed them to death, tearing these works of literature apart like we were slaughtering sheep. Only we didn't kill them for food. We killed them for fun, to display our superior intelligence, our vaunted wisdom. We were fools. We scraped the earth out from under our own discipline till all that was left was dust. I couldn't have said that then. I only knew I was sick to death of words. I couldn't bear the thought of spending the rest of my life with them. Then, two days before my degree ceremony, my parents—" He paused for a long moment before continuing. "They were driving down to Oxford for commencement and were killed in a motor-car smash."

"Oh, James!" Maggie reached across the stone wall and placed her hand on his arm.

He was silent for a long moment, and seemed not to hear her voice or feel her touch. Maggie had the sense that he was wrestling with something. Finally he continued, "When I heard the news, I got into my car and drove till I ran out of petrol." He pointed down the hill to the south. "My car stopped a quarter mile from Bill and Kezzy's. I walked to their house. Bill was out, but Kezzy invited me in, and by the time Bill returned, she had adopted me—I hardly know how it happened, even now. I never went back. I never want to. But"—he glanced at Maggie and gestured to the papers in her hand—"I realize I miss poetry. I might even be ready to read something other than the almanac and sheep breeding journals." He grinned at her, but there was sadness in his eyes.

Maggie squeezed his arm in sympathy. "Oh, James," she said again. "I'm so sorry."

He shrugged. "It was five years ago, Maggie. Time—you know."

"The great healer."

He nodded. "And earth. And wind. And sky." He grinned again. "And sheep."

Maggie looked out at the pasture, the sheep grazing placidly in the sun, the river wending silently in the middle distance, the green hills rising again on the other side. A breath of breeze touched her bare face and hands. Clutching E.B.'s sonnets, she desperately hoped James was right.

# 5

In ev'ry desert an oasis lies—
Its fruitful trees, viridescent springs seem
To thirsty sojourners' sand-blasted eyes
An Eden new—renewed—they think they dream—
As I do dream before this wicket gate—
A bench beneath plum-blossomed trees—
For me? Glad hand to latch I hesitate—
Might I sit in shadowed shade, drink in these
Pink petals? or do seraphs' swords of flame
Guard this gate? Is Eve scorned or welcomed here?
Might these trees' leaves heal haunted hearts self-shamed?
Might shamèd faces lift and feel no fear?
Might haunting flee? Hearts open to embrace?
Or will a further shaming mark this place?
                              —E.B., April 1818

❧

One afternoon in late October, mist shrouded the hills thicker than the dust indoors, but Maggie had to get out of the house. She and Gram had quarreled, and she needed air and space and rain on her face. She walked away from the river, toward town, where she thought she would be less likely to run into James; she needed solitude.

33

Over lunch Gram had asked, not for the first time, what Maggie's plan was, and Maggie, once again, said she didn't know. "You're going to run out of time if you wait too long," Gram had said, and Maggie had snapped, "I know that! Do you think I don't know that? Do you think I'm not aware every single day that my life has changed forever and that I need to decide what I'm going to do about it?"

The silence after this outburst had been excruciating. Maggie couldn't even finish her sandwich. She took it to the kitchen and left it there while she put on her jacket and boots and stormed out into the mist.

Gram was right, of course. She had to think about the future, figure out what she was going to do, but thinking of the future made her think of the past, and she desperately longed to forget the past, forget her foolishness in believing Brian had loved her. Would he have married her at all? Or had she been fooling herself in that, too?

She reached the edge of town and skirted it, keeping to the fields. Through the mist she saw a faint blur of yellow at the top of the next rise. A stand of birches, perhaps. She tromped toward it and thought of their final conversation, how she'd dreaded telling him over the phone—she'd wanted to see his face, wanted him to see hers—but what else could she do when he was in Atlanta and she in Spokane? She remembered how she'd told him she was pregnant, how there was a long and awful silence, how she'd said, "Brian?" and he'd said quietly, "This wasn't in my plans, Mag. Isn't there—you know—can't you do something about it?" Those were almost his last words to her; he never called again, was always "out" whenever she called him, and never returned her calls. Part of her was almost glad; it made it easier to vilify him, to feel justified in hating him. After her tenth—or maybe it was the twelfth—phone call, she'd given up. He went off to Yale Law in the fall; she came here. She had no reason to think she would ever see him again.

And to think she had loved him! How could she have been so blind, so stupid? She vacillated between hating him and hating herself. She called him the vilest names she could think of. Many times. And called herself quite a few at the same time. But all the name-calling in the world wouldn't change things.

The mist turned to rain. She felt it fall on her face as she reached the top of the hill and passed through the birches, their yellow leaves, the only color in sight, dropping silently onto the sodden ground. The fields were a grey and misty blur. She wasn't even sure where she was. She didn't care and, leaving the birches behind, kept walking.

She knew that if she didn't let go of her anger and hatred, she'd end up bitter and poisoned, like Dickens' Miss Havisham, surrounded only by her own moldy memories—all of them galling—and poisoning the souls of everyone around her, not least this child who now grew in her womb.

No, she would not choose that path. But how? How not to choose it? How to live without anger, without bitterness? How to choose joy and life and love in the face of rejection and betrayal? How did one do that? Had E.B. done it? Had she found a way to love her baby, to forgive its father? And if she had, how did she do it? Was James right, that it was just a matter of time? She didn't think so. Miss Havisham sat in that room in her wedding dress for decades. No, time alone was not enough. If she kept hating Brian, she would just keep hating Brian, and time would only make it worse. Unless she chose not to hate him.

Or herself.

She reached a stone wall and found she didn't have the strength to climb it, so she stood beside it, staring out across the rainy grey fields, lost to all but her swirling thoughts.

"Maggie!"

She started at the sound of James's voice, right beside her. Rain sheeted down the hood of his jacket.

"You're soaked through!" he said.

"Am I?" She looked down. Sure enough—her jacket was soaked, her jeans were soaked, even her boots were soaked. She hadn't noticed. She felt inside her pocket. E.B.'s sonnets were still there, but whether it was the pages or her hand that was wet, she could not tell.

James looked concerned. "Are you unwell?"

She shook her head. "No. No, I'm fine. Really. Just—distracted—that's all."

James grinned. "Must be some distraction to make you oblivious to rain like this."

"Yes. Yes, it is." She stared through the wet, grey air and suddenly felt cold.

"Come on," James said kindly, and offered her his arm. "I'll walk you home."

She felt fuzzy-headed and a bit dizzy. Everywhere she looked was grey. It seemed to take a long time to get back to the cottage. When they finally reached the gate, darkness was falling, and Maggie could hardly move her legs. In the dusky grey light, she noticed a bedraggled plum tree arcing its baring branches over the path to the door. Its leaves lay scattered and dingy on the pebbles of the path. As James lifted the latch and opened the gate, something joggled in Maggie's memory, but she was too cold and her brain too foggy to figure out what it was.

Firelight shone in the leaded panes of the window beside the door. James escorted her up the walk—propelled her, really—his hand on her elbow.

"Lily?" he called to Gram as he opened the front door.

Gram came into the room. "At last!" she exclaimed. "I've been worried sick!"

"She needs tea," James said.

"I'm fine, James, really," Maggie said, even as she felt herself sag dizzily against him.

"And dry clothes," he continued. "And something to eat."

Gram grabbed a blanket off the nearest chair and wrapped Maggie in it. "Thank you, James," she said as she led Maggie to a chair by the fire and sat her down. The door clicked softly closed behind them as James slipped back out into the falling night.

Maggie began to shake. She felt so cold. A sudden sob erupted from somewhere deep inside, and she realized she had not cried, not once, since the day she last talked to Brian. The tears came hard, and she let them, sobbing into her hands as Gram held her and stroked her wet hair and whispered, "Sh. Sh. It'll be all right. All shall be well, Maggie. Sh. All shall be well, dear. You'll see. All shall be well."

# 6

This place not Eden is but Promise Land—
Fertile fields, livestock, work, sweat on the brow
Of mother, father, son, whose open hands
Warm welcome did extend when 'neath the bough
Of apple-blossomed Jabbok I first passed
And stood upon their stoop in dusky gloam,
Atremble and alone. As Esau cast
Past wrongs to wind and welcomed Jacob home—
The prodigal returned—with tears, embrace,
And joy that bowed his brother to his knee
In awe at Esau's unexpected grace—
So these kind unknown kin did welcome me
To share their bread, to stand upon their sod,
Receive their care—their face the face of God.
                                    —E.B., June 1818

❧

The weeks passed. The days of soft sunshine alternated with days of low mists and fine rain and finally gave way to unremittingly grey skies.

By the middle of November, Maggie could no longer button her jeans. She'd been watching her belly thicken and knowing this day would come. But she was not going to buy special clothes, not until she absolutely had to. She used a rubber band to hold up her jeans. Then she placed her hands on her belly. What was going on in there? What did the baby look like now? When would she be able to feel him? Or was it a girl? A sudden rush of compassion filled her, and she started to cry. Again. Only this time she was crying not for herself but for this child growing within her, a child whose father had abandoned and rejected him. Yes, him. For she suddenly felt sure the baby was a boy.

*Poor kid*, she thought. *What a horrible way to start life.*

And in that moment she realized that she hadn't loved him, either. She had seen him as an inconvenience, an interruption, a mistake.

She was not much better than Brian.

She closed her eyes and vowed that this child would not grow up knowing himself abandoned and rejected. No. She would make sure her baby was loved. And she would start by loving him herself. Only she didn't know how. How could you feel something you did not feel? And then she remembered a book she'd read last year, in which one of the characters had said that love was not some wonderful thing that you feel but some hard thing that you do.

Maggie could do hard things: she had been in crew for three years; she had hiked the Wonderland Trail with her father. She could love this baby, and she would. She placed her hands on her belly and whispered, "Hey there. I'm Maggie. I'm your mama."

The baby didn't suddenly kick. Maggie's feelings didn't suddenly change. *For heaven's sake,* she told herself with a rueful look in the mirror. *What did you expect? You haven't so much as felt the baby move yet. Did you expect him to suddenly leap for joy in your womb, like you're the Virgin Mary or something?*

Shaking her head at her own foolishness, she left her room and went down to the kitchen to help Gram with breakfast before they headed back upstairs to sort through Helen's things.

By lunchtime, the clouds had lifted; they were high in the sky and light grey instead of dark and lowering. Maggie wrapped a scarf around her neck, donned her jacket and boots, and tromped outdoors with a thermos of hot tea, a blanket, and E.B.'s copy of *Paradise Lost* in her backpack. She found a sheltered corner in the angle of two stone walls that looked out over the Land of Counterpane. She wrapped herself in the blanket, pulled out the book, and began to read.

She had reached the temptation scene: the serpent was coiled up like a tower, preparing his assault on Eve, and Maggie felt nervous. She knew the choice Eve would make, but still she found herself hoping that somehow, this time, it would be different, that somehow Eve would not be deceived.

"Good book?"

She started at the sound of James's voice beside her.

"I think you delight in doing that," Maggie said wryly.

"Sorry," he said with a grin as he dropped onto the ground beside her. But he didn't look sorry. "You're about as jumpy as one of my sheep."

"Do you like frightening them, too?"

He shook his head. "I do not."

"Well, I guess that makes me special, then, though I'm not sure I feel complimented."

He laughed, and she found herself laughing, too. Inclining his head toward the book she held, he asked, "What are you reading?"

"*Paradise Lost*. I found this copy in the attic at Helen's. Isn't it beautiful?"

She handed it to him, and a shadow seemed to pass over his face. He looked away from her, looked down at the book in his hands. He held it gently, almost gingerly, like he was afraid of damaging it.

Maggie wondered what he was thinking, but she waited quietly. He had never pried into her life, and she would not pry into his.

"I miss Milton," he said at length. "I never thought I would. But I do, and I'm glad. Until I wrote my thesis on him, he was my favorite." He opened the book to the place Maggie had placed her bookmark.

"I'd never read anything by him," she said, "except that famous sonnet—you know, 'When I consider how my light is spent.'"

James nodded. "A great sonnet. One of the greatest." He shrugged. "But I might be biased."

Maggie smiled and gestured at the book, open in his hand. "I'm kind of enthralled by *Paradise Lost*. It baffles me how he can write a story I know so well, and I still find myself hoping it's going to end differently. I want Eve to make the right choice."

"That's part of his brilliance, enabling us to get inside her skin so fully that we don't know the end of the story because so far as Eve is concerned, it hasn't been written yet." James rested his arm on his knee and gazed off into the distance. "But we also remain ourselves, and we know the decision she makes. It's that tension between freedom and fate that makes us hold our breath in hope and fear."

Maggie stared at him. "Yes," she said slowly. He was exactly right. She was holding her breath in hope and fear, and not just for Eve. She thought of E.B., and of herself, of the decisions she'd made and must still make, and she felt suddenly vulnerable.

A drop of rain fell onto her cheek. She pulled up her hood. James closed *Paradise Lost* and handed it back to her. "It's a beautiful copy," he said as she tucked it into her backpack.

❧

In mid-December Maggie and Gram finished clearing out the attic and celebrated with a week off before moving on to the upstairs bedrooms that were almost as full of stuff as the attic had been.

Maggie's belly swelled until one day she could no longer even use a rubber band to hold up her jeans. "Well, little man," she said to the baby, "looks like you're growing. And it looks like I'm going to need some new clothes."

Gram took to her to the nearest town with a department store, an hour's drive away, so she could buy jeans with an elastic waistband. In the dressing room, Maggie laughed at her reflection. "Kid," she said, "you're making me look ridiculous."

But that night, lying in bed, she felt the baby's first kick, and a thrill shot from her belly straight through her heart to her head. Her eyes filled with tears of wonder and joy.

It pricked her conscience every now and again that she had not yet told James. She knew she should, but she didn't know how. "Oh, by the way, sorry I didn't mention it sooner, but I'm pregnant." It was too awkward, and the longer she waited the more awkward it became, especially since she suspected that her feelings for him were not strictly friendly, a suspicion she had no intention of exploring and did her best to ignore altogether. She shrugged her feelings, and her guilt, away. At some point, he would know. Some days she thought he must already knew— baggy shirts and bulky sweaters could only hide a bulging belly for so long—but he never by word or look intimated that he knew.

Three days before Christmas Maggie sat down at the desk in the attic to wrap E.B.'s copy of *Paradise Lost*. She wrote "For James" on the flyleaf and then sat for a long while staring out the window, unsure what else to write. Finally she added, "With gratitude for your friendship, Maggie."

It was starting to snow, so she bundled the gift-wrapped book into a wool blanket, which she stowed in her backpack. Then she went in search of James.

As she tromped through Helen's fields, her boots crunched the thin layer of snow on the grass. She clambered over a stile in one of the stone walls that bordered a pasture, dropped to the ground, and stopped. Not twenty paces down the hill from where she stood a sheep lay on its back, its legs sticking straight up in the air. She had never seen a sheep in this position, and she wondered if it was hurt, or just sleeping. She walked slowly over—she didn't want to frighten it—and realized she knew this sheep. It was a Ryeland that she'd nicknamed Brown Betty.

Brown Betty looked up at Maggie and kicked her legs half-heartedly. What did that mean? Did she want Maggie to leave? Or was she in distress? Maggie looked around, but she and Brown Betty were alone in the field. No James, and not even another sheep, in sight. Maggie didn't know what to do.

Then she noticed that Brown Betty was lying in her own droppings. Surely she wouldn't do that if she weren't hurt. She bent down and gently placed her hand on the sheep's head. "I'm going to get help," she said. Brown Betty looked steadily up at her and blinked, and Maggie felt as if the sheep recognized her, and trusted her. "I'll be right back," she promised.

Turning, she raced across the field and over another wall,

scanning that pasture for James. She slipped in the snow but caught herself before she fell. On she ran, surprised at how breathless she was, through one field after another, and finally found him in the furthest Stonewold pasture, spreading hay from an open shed onto the ground, sheep pushing around him. She waved to him, and he waved back before bending to his work again. She continued running across the field. He grabbed a bale of hay out of the shed and set it on the ground. She reached him just as he was cutting the twine that held it together.

"Brown Betty," she gasped.

He straightened and gave her a puzzled look. Snowflakes dotted his woolen cap and the shoulders of his coat.

"Brown Betty," she said again, holding her side and trying to catch her breath.

"What?" James spread the hay from the bale on the ground for the sheep. They pushed at him, and at her, too.

"The brown Ryeland. I call her Brown Betty."

"Really?" He grinned.

"She's—I think she's hurt."

The grin vanished. "Where?"

"Back there." Maggie pointed in the direction she'd come.

"Show me."

Maggie led the way back across the fields, moving as fast as she could and huffing in a most embarrassing way. Clearly pregnancy was affecting her lungs as well as the rest of her body.

Snow continued to fall slowly in big soft flakes, dusting the fields with white and settling on the tops of the stone walls.

Finally they reached the pasture where Maggie had left Brown Betty. "There," she said, pointing.

"She's cast," James said, hurrying across the field.

"Cast?"

"Stuck on her back. Like a tortoise. She can't get back up without help. It's good you came to get me. Cast sheep will die if they're not put back on their feet." James bent over Brown Betty, grabbed one of her hooves, and pulled her onto her side. The sheep struggled into a kneeling position, her legs bent under her. Then she staggered to her feet and fell right back down.

Maggie sucked in a sharp breath. "Is she all right?"

"She will be. It'll just take her a moment to find her footing."

Maggie watched as Brown Betty pushed herself into a half-standing position, her back legs straight, her front legs still bent beneath her. She stumbled again, losing her footing. On her third try she managed to get to her feet. She stood still and seemed to Maggie to be trembling.

"Is she all right now?"

"Aye. We'll wait another minute, see if she can walk."

Brown Betty shuddered and shook her head rapidly back and forth. Then she took a step, stumbled, righted herself, and staggered sideways.

"She's a bit wobbly," James said. "Not surprising. I expect she was lying there rather a long while."

"How did that happen?" Maggie asked. "Her getting cast?"

"She probably lay on her side and then accidentally rolled down the hill here and got stuck on her back. It sometimes happens if a sheep's fleece gets wet or muddy, which makes it heavy, or when they're about to lamb."

Maggie and James watched Brown Betty slowly regain her footing.

"She's my favorite," Maggie said.

"Really? Why's that?"

Maggie smiled ruefully. "Probably because she's the only one

I recognize. She looks different from the others." She shrugged. "And I like to think that she recognizes me, too. She certainly seems to."

James grinned. "We'll make a shepherdess of you yet."

Despite the cold, Maggie felt her cheeks grow warm, and for a moment she could not think what to say, but then she remembered that she had come out to bring him a gift. She slung her backpack off her shoulder and pulled out the blanket. "I have a Christmas present for you."

"That's a very nice blanket," James said with another grin. "Thank you."

Maggie grinned back. "The gift is inside the blanket, silly. I didn't want it to get wet." She handed him the wrapped book. James started to unwrap it, but Maggie stopped him. "Don't open it now. Wait till you're someplace dry."

James held the package in his gloved hands. "Is it—?"

"Don't guess," Maggie interrupted. But she could tell he'd already guessed. The grin on his face gave it away.

"Thank you, Maggie."

She smiled back at him. "You're welcome."

His smile faded, and he looked a little distressed. "I—I'm sorry. I didn't get you a present."

"You didn't have to." She smiled. "It's nice to feel like I'm giving you something without receiving anything in return."

James gave her a quizzical look. Maggie glanced at the ground, hoping she hadn't communicated more than she meant to and wishing she had held her tongue. She forced herself to smile. "Don't open it till you're someplace dry," she said again, shoving the blanket into her backpack. She looked across the pasture to where Brown Betty walked slowly away from them, her gait steady. "She'll be all right?"

"Thanks to you, aye, she'll be just fine."

Maggie nodded and turned to go.

"I'll walk with you back to Helen's," James said.

"You don't have to do that."

"I know I don't have to. I want to. I like your company."

Maggie swallowed.

"Besides," he added with a grin, "there are some sheep in your fields that I have to feed."

"I see." Maggie laughed. "All right, then. I'll help you."

"Deal."

❧

January brought more gray weather, more rain mixed with the occasional snow, and more and harder kicks from the baby.

One rainy afternoon in the middle of the month Maggie accompanied James back to the Jordans' barn, where he began to fill the feed boxes while she fondled the small ears and stroked the soft head of Brown Betty.

She'd had another difficult conversation with Gram over lunch. "You need to decide what you're going to do, Maggie," Gram had said gently but firmly. "You only have two more months to find adoptive parents, if that's the path you're going to take."

It was the path Gram wanted her to take, Maggie knew, and the path her parents wanted her to take as well. Then she could go back to school and finish her degree, go back to her old life as if she really were just larking in England this year.

James's voice broke the silence. "My parents weren't the only ones killed in that motor-car smash," he said.

Maggie jerked her head up to look at him. It took her a

moment to register what he'd said. Then a knot of foreboding formed in her chest.

"My wife was in the car, too. We had just found out she was expecting. We were going to announce it at my graduation party."

Maggie's eyes filled with tears, and the knot in her chest turned into a stone that weighed on her heart. "Oh, James." She crossed the stall and took his hands in hers. "Oh, James," she said again, her voice a broken whisper. "I'm so, so sorry."

His eyes were misty as he said, "It was five years ago, Maggie. Time—" His voice cracked.

She nodded. "I know. The great healer."

Brown Betty butted her head against Maggie's backside. She smiled through her tears. "And sheep help, too."

James smiled back, a little sadly. "Are they helping you?"

Maggie's smile faded. She released his hands and patted Brown Betty's head. "What do you mean?" she said, even though she was pretty sure she knew exactly what he meant.

"You're pregnant," he said, matter-of-factly.

Maggie couldn't speak. She could only stand there, awkward and ashamed, feeling her face drain of color.

"When were you planning to tell me?"

Maggie kept her eyes on Brown Betty. "I wasn't," she finally said, softly. "I figured you'd figure it out eventually." She shrugged. "And you did."

A long silence followed, the only sounds the rustle of the sheep as they rummaged in the feed boxes.

Maggie finally hazarded a look at James. He was studying her, his face inscrutable, and she looked quickly back down at Brown Betty. Was he angry? No, she realized, he was not angry. He had just told her about his wife. She understood why he had not told her sooner. It was the same reason she had never mentioned the baby or Brian. And she understood why he chose to tell her now. It felt like an apology, and forgiveness, and an invitation.

"We met my freshman year in college." She sat down on a nearby hay bale, and James sat down beside her. Keeping her eyes on Brown Betty, she briefly told him the whole story. "So Brian went off to Yale, and I came here," she concluded.

James did not say that Brian was a jerk or that she was better off without him, for which Maggie was thankful. He only placed a gentle hand on her arm and said, "I'm sorry, Maggie. You deserved better."

They sat for a long moment, his hand on her arm offering her silent assurance of his presence and care. His fingers, she noticed, were long and lean, like his face, his whole frame, long and lean and strong. He gave her arm a gentle squeeze before he stood and returned to feeding the sheep. "Has it been long enough?"

"Long enough?"

"For time—you know." He gestured to Brown Betty. "And sheep."

Maggie ran her hand across Brown Betty's back. "I think so. A little. I'm not so angry as I was. Some days—some days I'm even happy, when I don't think about the future. Gram says I need to think about the future, that I need to decide what I'm going to do." She rested a hand on her belly. "But whenever I think about it, I feel afraid, because I don't know what to do."

James was silent for a moment. "I don't know about that, Maggie. I think you do know what to do—or at least what you want to do. You're only afraid to do it."

Maggie started to protest, but the words died on her lips.

49

*Did* she know what she wanted? Gram and her parents wanted her to give this baby up for adoption. Brian had wanted her to abort it. What did *she* want? She wanted to stop loving people to the point of wrecking herself. She wanted to stop giving them what they wanted at her own expense. Love, she had always known, was costly. But she realized now that it was a costliness that filled you, as this baby was filling her, not a costliness that left you bereft of yourself. She looked at James, filling the feed bins with hay. He had loved much—and lost much. Love had cost him—deeply—but he still had himself—his strength of character, his kindness, his sense of humor, his gentleness. He could have chosen bitterness—his parents, wife, and unborn child—*Oh God*, Maggie thought, tears swimming in her eyes at the thought of all he had lost. But he honored his love for them by remaining himself, by continuing to live, by learning to laugh again, to love again—the Jordans, Helen, Floss, his sheep, even, Maggie thought, herself, a little, as a friend, and maybe—but she slammed the door on that thought.

James was right. She knew what she wanted to do. She only lacked courage to do it.

"James?" she said, standing and brushing hay off her jeans. "I'm going to go. There's a difficult conversation I need to have, and I want to get it over with before I lose my nerve."

James smiled as if to say *good for you*. "I'm almost done. I'll walk you home. It's nearly dark out."

Maggie knew better than to protest. James MacKinnon would never let a pregnant woman walk home across wet fields in the dark, especially if she was headed there to face her future. She did not want to protest. She welcomed his company.

# 7

This Promise Land of plenty is not mine.
A foreigner I feel, a Moabite
At table eating Boaz' food and wine—
I cannot raise my face to meet your sight.
Would I were blameless, good, like loyal Ruth,
I'd clasp your feet upon the threshing floor—
No shame would mar my countenance; the truth
And faith and firmness of my state would pour
Like water, shine like light, from out my eyes
And you would wake and see and smile and stroke
My face—your work-worn hands, so kind and wise,
Would gather me beneath your garment's yoke.
I am no Ruth but Rahab scarlet stained—
In dreams alone is such a future gained.

        —E.B., August 1818

&#10087;

The day after Maggie called her parents and told them what they did not want to hear, the fields were swathed in thick mist from dawn till dusk. Her conversations with Gram and her parents the night before had exhausted her, and the dark grey light made her sleepy, so after lunch, instead of going for her usual walk, she took a nap.

That evening, as she washed up the dinner dishes, she could hear rain still splattering on the windows and occasionally hissing in the fire in the parlour. The baby kicked, hard enough to take her breath away for a moment. Only eight more weeks until her life changed forever.

No, her life had changed forever last July when she realized she was pregnant. She found she was no longer angry. Would she really have wanted never to come here? Never to know the feel of the wind from the river on her face or the blue of the sky above the emerald of the fields? Would she wish away these months with Gram, hearing her stories of growing up on these hills? Or the privilege of sorting through a century of her family's belongings, touching each one, learning more about who she was because of this place she'd come from? Would she want never to have discovered E.B.'s sonnets? Not to have spent hours puzzling over who she was and what her story was? Never to have met James? Her heart shrank at the thought.

One by one she pulled the plates out of the rinse water and set them on the drying rack. No, she could not wish away these past months, no matter how dramatically her life had changed, or was about to change. She wondered if E.B. had felt that same way. Had she felt glad somehow for the pain and shame she endured because of where it brought her in the end? In this house, she had met compassion and kindness. Here, she had loved— someone—probably the son mentioned in the fifth sonnet. Did he love her in return? What had happened to him? What had happened to her? To her baby?

Gram had said all those months ago that there was a family Bible around here somewhere. Perhaps it held a clue to E.B.'s identity, to her future, but they still hadn't unearthed it. Maggie wondered if it even existed anymore.

A knock sounded on the kitchen door. She dried her hands on a dish towel and went to answer it.

James stood on the stoop, dripping. "I didn't see you today, and I wanted—" He looked around and lowered his voice. "I wanted to hear how your conversations went yesterday."

Maggie invited him in and put the kettle on for tea. As they waited for the water to boil, she finished rinsing the dishes and told him of her conversation with Gram, which had gone far better than she'd expected. And her parents, though disappointed, had borne the news with remarkable calm. "They're concerned, of course," she said, drying her hands. "This isn't the path they imagined for me." The kettle whistled and she poured the water into the teapot. "It isn't the path I imagined for myself." She rested her hands on her belly, gently, tenderly.

James said, "I never imagined I'd become a sheep farmer—not in a million years."

Maggie glanced up at him. He was looking at her hands on her belly. She wondered if he were thinking of his own unborn child, of the life he might have had, and in that moment the thing that she had refused to acknowledge, that had been growing inside her right along with this baby, blazed up in her, a quiet, steady flame. This time she did not put it out. When James met her gaze, a question in his eyes, her smile was a little wobbly, but she took his hand and rested it on her belly. After a moment, the baby kicked, a one-two punch that made them both grin.

"Sometimes," James said quietly, "the path chooses us, and it turns out to be every bit as good as what we'd have chosen for ourselves."

❧

It continued to rain for three days. The river rose, half the roads were flooded out, and power lines and phone lines were down all over the county. Isolated from the world by flood and phone failure, Gram and Maggie finished cleaning one of the upstairs bedrooms, the one closest to Maggie's. She smiled as she scrubbed the last of the dust from the floor planks. It would make a fine room for the baby, once there were curtains in the window and a rug on the floor. There was already a crib in the corner, and a rocking chair. Helen had thrown away nothing, it seemed, and Maggie was increasingly glad of that.

After supper on the third day, when the rain was coming down harder than ever—the fire in the parlour hissed loudly every few seconds as a raindrop made its way down the chimney and into the flames—Gram had gone upstairs with a headache and a cup of tea, and Maggie sat quietly on the sofa, watching the fire dance and sing. A knock on the kitchen door pulled her from her reverie. She heaved herself off the sofa and went to answer it.

"James!" she cried when she saw him, drenched and dripping, on the stoop. "You're soaked through!" She stepped aside and gestured him into the kitchen. "What on earth possessed you to come out on a night like this?"

"I haven't seen you in three days." He shrugged off his coat and hung it on a peg by the door. "I missed you."

It wasn't just the words. It was the tone, the tenderness of it. Maggie's heart lurched into her throat and she found that she could not speak. It took several swallows to return it to its proper place. "Come," she was finally able to say, and led the way into the parlour. "Sit by the fire and dry off. I'll make you a cup of tea."

When the tea was ready, Maggie brought it and the cups on a tray to the parlor and set them on the low table in front of the sofa. She found that she could not look at James as he crossed the room to sit down beside her, and that her hand trembled a little as she poured the tea.

They sat in silence, sipping their tea and staring into the fire. But after a few moments Maggie found she did not mind. The silence was strangely comforting, and she slowly ceased to be aware of it. She finished her tea, set down her teacup, and leaned back on the sofa. The fire hissed and popped. The baby stirred. James reached over and clasped Maggie's hand in his.

Her heart slammed into her ribs at his touch, and she looked at him sharply, but he was still gazing into the fire, seemingly unconscious of what he had just done.

"James?" she said after a moment.

"Aye?"

"You're holding my hand."

A smile played at the corners of his mouth, but he still did not look at her. "Aye. Does it bother you?"

"No," Maggie said slowly. In fact, she rather liked it. If the tattooing of her heart was any indication, she liked it a lot. "But I'd like to know what you mean by it."

He looked at her then. "I mean to marry you if you'll let me."

For one moment all the air seemed sucked out of the room. Maggie felt plastered in place. She could neither breathe nor speak nor think. Then—"Marry me! But we—you—I—I'm pregnant! And—and you—you don't know me well enough!"

James squeezed her hand. "I know you're pregnant. I've known it almost as long as I've known you—ever since the day

55

you showed me those sonnets that you've been carrying around in your pocket."

Maggie felt her cheeks flame.

"And I've spent part of almost every day for the past six months with you, Maggie. I know you well enough to know that you're brave and adventurous and loyal and kind. I've seen the way you treat your Gram, the way you treat Floss and the sheep. I've seen the way you've wrestled silently with your anger toward Brian and never once maligned him."

"But I have! Oh James, you don't know how hateful my thoughts toward him have been!"

"But you're not giving in to those thoughts, Maggie. Of course they're there, but you're fighting them—you're wrestling them to the ground and pinning them there. You're not letting them rob you of laughter and joy and love. You love that baby— and—I think you love me—perhaps not as much as I love you— perhaps not in the same way—"

"Oh, James." Maggie's voice was a teary whisper.

"I know that marrying a Scottish sheep-farmer wasn't in your plans, Maggie, any more than moving to England or having a baby was in your plans. It certainly wasn't in my plans to fall in love with a poetry-loving American lass and her baby. But you've become part of the fabric of my life, Maggie; you've woven yourself right into it."

"Oh, James," she said again, still teary but almost smiling.

James squeezed her hand again and rested his other hand on her cheek. "I love you, Mary Magdalen Lowell. Be my wife?"

Maggie's heart was thumping so hard she could barely speak. "Oh, James."

"You've said that three times now, Maggie. Do you think you could say something else?"

Maggie grinned through her tears. "Yes," she whispered.
"Yes?"
"Yes."

# 8

Maggie and James were married quietly, two weeks later, before the hearth in Helen's house. Besides the parish priest, only Gram, Bill, and Kezzy were present.

James moved into the house with his few belongings— Maggie could hardly believe how few. Some clothes, a box of books about farming and raising sheep, and the beautiful little copy of *Paradise Lost* that she had given him for Christmas. That was all. She saw little more of him than she had before. He was up before dawn to head down to Stonewold—the first of the ewes were lambing—and out all day and most of the night, too, though most days he came home for lunch and again for supper.

Home.

Maggie smiled at the word. This was home now, for both of them.

In mid-February, as she and Gram were cleaning out the middle bedroom upstairs, Maggie pulled several boxes out of the small closet and began sifting through their contents. Books mostly—cheap, yellowing paperbacks and school yearbooks, if that's what they were called over here—and a few photographs of people she didn't recognize wearing horrid clothes from the '70's. At the bottom of the box was a dusty velveteen bag, and inside the bag—

Maggie gasped as she pulled out a large, heavy book. "Gram!" she called. "Gram! I've found it!"

"Found what, dear?" Gram looked up from the pile of clothes she was tossing, one at a time, into a garbage bag.

"The Bible!" It was a deep mahogany color, with the words Holy Bible etched deeply into the boards, which were fastened with a brass clasp. Maggie's fingers trembled as she opened it. Gram crossed the room and lowered herself onto the floor beside Maggie. Together they slowly turned the pages, old and brittle, and breathed the faint but wonderful scent of old books that the pages gave off. It had been well-loved, Maggie could tell. The corners of the cover were worn, and the pages, tinged with yellow, bore unmistakable marks of having been read and turned—a smudge in the corner, a faint outline of a fingerprint. Generations of her family had held this book in their hands.

At the front of the Bible were several pages of a family tree. The last entry was the birth of Maggie's grandfather, George Lowell. "They didn't even mark down your marriage to him, Gram," Maggie said. "I wonder why."

Gram shrugged. "Perhaps the Bible was already in this box. Though why they'd have packed it away I don't know."

Maggie ran her finger lightly up the Lowell family tree. George's parents, Helen James and Jared Lowell, married in 1906.

Jared's parents, Margaret Wright and Henry Lowell, married in 1879.

Henry's parents, Jane Elliott and another George Lowell—*Was Grandpa named for him?* Maggie wondered—married in 1836.

George's parents, Elizabeth Bradford and Samuel Lowell, married in 1818.

1818. Maggie's eyes went wide. Elizabeth Bradford.

"E.B.," she whispered. "Oh, Gram, I've found her."

"Found whom, dear?"

"E.B. Remember? I asked about her—last fall—when I found the—" She caught herself just in time. "The books. In that trunk. In the attic."

Gram nodded. "Oh, yes, I do remember. So the books were hers, were they?" She looked at where Maggie's finger rested on the family tree. "She died in 1889. 100 years ago next month."

Footsteps sounded on the stairs. "James!" Maggie called. "James! Come here! Come look!"

As James entered the room, Gram held up her hands to him. "Be a dear and help an old woman to her feet," she said, and he did. She gave him a kiss on the cheek. "I'm going to go make lunch."

"We'll be right down, Gram," Maggie called after her. "James, look!" She pointed to Elizabeth Bradford's name. "I found E.B. She's my—" She quickly counted the generations. "My great-great-great-great grandmother."

James sat on the floor beside her, one leg behind her back, an arm across her shoulders.

"He married her, James. See?" She pointed to Samuel Lowell's name.

"1818," James said, scanning the other names and dates. "It's the only marriage with just a year. No month, no day."

"He was protecting her," Maggie said softly, tears welling in her eyes. "And legitimizing her child."

Her heart seemed to swell in her chest. E.B. had known love, the caring protection of Samuel Lowell. As Samuel was the only son of his parents, Maggie thought he must be the son mentioned in the fifth sonnet—"mother, father, son"—and also the man with whom E.B. had fallen in love, the man to whom she had written the sixth sonnet. Maggie wondered what it cost

60

Samuel Lowell, in that day and age, to marry a woman who was pregnant with another man's child.

"They named him George Samuel," James was saying, "after Samuel and his father."

They must have been very loving people, Maggie thought, to take in this young woman, to consent to their son's marrying her, to record the birth of her child as their own grandson, and with his grandfather's name.

"They had four more children," James said, "three boys and a girl."

Maggie looked at the family tree, at the names James was pointing at, and another thought struck her. "Samuel had three sons of his own, but still he left the farm to George," she said. "If he hadn't, I wouldn't be here. It would belong to some distant cousin somewhere." Tears spilled down her cheeks.

It could have been so different—if E.B. had never come to this house—if Samuel had not married her—or not treated her son as his own—if James's wife hadn't died in that horrible car crash—if he hadn't run out of gas just over the hill—if Brian hadn't been such a prat—if any one thing had been different— she would never have come here—or James would never have come here—their paths would never have crossed—they would never have met. "It feels like a miracle," she whispered, her throat aching.

"It's not a miracle, Maggie," James said tenderly. "He loved that boy, and love is stronger than blood."

She leaned her head against his shoulder. "I think that's a miracle, too."

A month later Maggie took down the Bible from its new place on a shelf in the parlour. In the days after she'd found it, she'd brought the family tree up to date, right up to her and James's marriage. Tonight she was going to record the birth of Samuel James MacKinnon.

A fire crackled quietly in the hearth. Upstairs she could hear Gram walking across the hall to her room, and the squeak of a floorboard as she lay down on her bed. Otherwise the room was quiet.

She set the Bible on the low table in front of the sofa, where James lay crashed out with Sam cradled against his side. Babies were exhausting, that was certain. She had never been so tired in her life, or so happy. She perched on the edge of the sofa and smiled at her husband and her son, and her heart so ached with love and gladness that it brought tears to her eyes.

As she pulled the Bible into her lap, she lost her grip on it, and it fell to the floor with a dull thud, the clasp releasing, and the book falling open on the rag rug. Maggie's hand flew to her chest for a moment before she gathered the Bible up, hoping she hadn't damaged it. She set it back on the table and saw that its pages had fallen open to the first chapter of Matthew. Wedged into the spine was a folded square of paper, yellow with age. She stared at it. Then, with trembling fingers, she picked it up. "James," she whispered. "James."

He turned his face toward her, his eyes half-open.

She held the paper up. "I think—I think it's another of E.B.'s sonnets."

James smiled and squeezed her free hand. "You already know how her story ended," he said gently. "Why don't you open it and read it?"

Maggie nodded. Slowly she unfolded the paper, swallowed the lump in her throat, and read.

❧

No Mary am I, but Joseph you are—
To see beyond my sin and fear and shame
And place upon my finger your ringed star
And shelter me, my child beneath your name.
As Rahab was by Zalmon loved, though she
Was crimson as the cord that saved her kin—
As Boaz sheltered Ruth, redeemed to be
His wife—Hosea loved despite her sin
His faithless wife, and faithful did remain—
So God above His people loved, and loves
Us still. However far we flee in pain
And shame and sunken rage, He moves
To seek and find and hold and heal—His grace
A vast and wide and high and deep embrace.
                                        —E.B.L., October 1818

# Being Grace Kelly

On her 18th birthday, when she was finally able to, Margaret Kelly, who had been called Daisy her entire life—to distinguish her from her mother who was also Margaret Kelly—went down to the Courthouse and legally changed her name to Grace.

She had been planning this event since she was 14 and saw her first Grace Kelly film, *To Catch a Thief.* She'd watched it because it starred her hero, Cary Grant. But in less than two hours, Grace Kelly eclipsed him. Daisy had always thought "Daisy Kelly" was a silly name, completely unsuited to her. It was a sunny name, vivacious and bright, and Daisy was quiet, more like the moon than the sun. As a name, Grace Kelly was far more appropriate, regal and elegant and understated. When she grew up, Daisy decided, she was going to be Grace Kelly.

She watched every Grace Kelly movie she could get her hands on and studied the way she talked and walked and what she wore. She read Grace Kelly biographies. She started taking drama classes and auditioned for each school play. When she wasn't cast (and sometimes when she was), she worked behind the scenes, mostly in the costume shop, where she learned to sew, and she loved it: she could make her own Grace Kelly-style clothes. Whenever she found herself in a situation and she didn't know what to do, she asked herself, "What would Grace Kelly do?" and she'd do it…because, after all, she was Grace Kelly… or she soon would be.

On the morning of May 4, 1988, one month before high school graduation, she skipped her first two classes, went down to the courthouse, and changed her name.

For 25 years, she never looked back.

She went to college and majored in Fashion and Theatre. She never became one of the flamboyant drama types who populated the college theatre. She didn't want to be one. She was warm and kind, but she preferred to remain a little apart from the whole thing, present but retaining part of herself for herself alone, quietly keeping most of her thoughts and feelings to herself. She slowly came to see those qualities as strengths she could draw on when she was acting. "Still waters run deep," one of her directors once said. She smiled inwardly whenever she remembered those words.

Upon graduation, she stayed in town, working in local theatres, both onstage and in the costume shop. She acted in a few independent movies, too, shot by directors she knew from the theatre scene. A few of her college chums had gone to Hollywood; they wrote to Grace, telling her she needed to come down, too. But she had no Hollywood ambitions. When she was still in high school, she'd read somewhere that the original Grace Kelly had said Hollywood was the saddest place she'd ever been. And from what Grace could see, it was truer now than it had been when the first Grace Kelly said it. Alcoholism and drug abuse and broken relationships seemed part and parcel of that scene, and she wanted none of it. Her own parents had celebrated their 25th wedding anniversary during Grace's sophomore year in college; she wanted that sort of stability and the happiness they shared for herself and her own someday children.

She was under no illusions that she'd marry an honest-to-God prince, but she'd been telling herself since she was 14 that she *would* marry a prince among men. The first time she saw her future husband she didn't even really see him. He was just one in the line of actors she was measuring for their costumes. He probably talked to her. Knowing him, he would have, but she didn't remember. Her mind was on her work. It wasn't till later that she even noticed him. And then, only because he was different from the other actors she knew, most of whom, while delightful in many ways, were either wildly insecure or obnoxiously full of themselves. She understood that dichotomy herself; she'd lived it, but she lived it internally. Grace Kelly was always modulated and discreet. She didn't let her insecurities show like so many open wounds, nor did she flaunt her abilities. She let them speak for themselves. And if no one noticed, neither would they see that it pained her. And, eventually, it stopped paining her. She received the praise and friendship of colleagues and directors who appreciated that she was a professional, and she learned not to care too much about the rest. And she had no desire to attach herself to anyone who could not do the same.

Ronald could, even though he was very different from her—more outgoing, more easygoing, but never flamboyant or outrageous. He conversed as easily with the directors and leading actors as he did with the stagehands and ushers, and with the same deference, as if he genuinely thought they were his equals, or even his betters, every last one of them. It was this that made Grace first notice him, his genuine amiableness. No one used words like amiable anymore, and it was, she thought, a pity, because it was the perfect word to describe him.

After she'd worked with him on three different shows over the course of a year, she was smitten. But she never let it show. She was Grace Kelly, and she did not wear her heart on her sleeve. When Ronald finally, as he put it later, "worked up the nerve" and asked her out, she smiled a perfectly serene smile and said she'd be pleased to have dinner with him. One dinner led to two, and by the end of the third dinner, Grace was as head over heels in love as any character she had ever played.

After six or seven or ten dinners, when it was clear that Ronald enjoyed her company as much as she enjoyed his, she decided it was time to tell him that Grace Kelly wasn't the name she'd been given at birth. So she casually mentioned over their next dinner together that she used to be called Daisy.

He raised an eyebrow. "That's surprising. It hardly suits you."

She felt mildly triumphant. "Exactly. It never suited me, which is why I changed my name to Grace."

He smiled. "Grace suits you perfectly."

And that was all, until shortly after their engagement, after he'd met her brother and sister and her parents who, after ten years, still insisted on calling her Daisy. He asked, over coffee at her apartment, "Why Grace? There are a lot of other names out there, and Grace Kelly was…"

"Already taken?"

"Yes, I guess that's what I was getting at. Why Grace Kelly?"

She twisted her napkin in her lap. "Because when I was a teenager, I wanted to be her. Daisy Kelly seemed such a silly name. Even now, it seems to belong to a stranger, someone I never was. But I could be Grace Kelly. I don't look like her, I know, but I act like her. I *am* like her. Taking her name was the first step toward becoming the person I knew I could be, the person I knew I already was, if only I could be shed of Daisy and the bright twinkliness of that name. I'm not bright and twinkly. I never have been. I never wanted to be. I wanted to be graceful and gracious." She gave a small smile. "I wanted to be Grace."

He reached across the sofa and squeezed her hand. "And you are, darling." For a moment they were both silent and simply looked at each other. Then he said, "I suppose, once we're married, you're going to want to call me Rainier."

She widened her eyes. "May I?"

At his horrified expression, she burst into merry laughter. His horror evaporated into relief, and he tackled her, tickling and kissing her at the same time. After several moments, the tickling subsided and only the kissing remained. And several moments after that, he whispered, "I love you, Grace." She thought they might be the only words she would ever want to hear.

They married and had children—two girls and a boy—and led the unconventional life of actors, sheltering their children in the circle of their love and zealously guarding the flame of their love for each other; neither of them wanted it to go out, and they knew, given the difficulty of the life they'd chosen, that keeping that flame alive would require work and sacrifice, and they undertook both with joy, choosing gratefulness that they had each other to love, and work they both loved, and children they both loved.

With so much to love, Grace wondered, how could she ever be unhappy? But she was, sometimes.

"Everyone is, sometimes," Ronald reminded her.

"Even you?"

He cocked her a grin. "Yes, even I, happy heart that I have, am sometimes unhappy."

But the unhappy times never lasted long. Work required

attention. The children required attention. And attention to something else left little room for unhappiness. It withered, slowly, and suddenly Grace would realize she was content once more.

Days passed and weeks and months and years. The children grew. Her parents aged. And one day Grace got a call from her father. Her mother had been diagnosed with ALS. She drove home that day. Her mother was in better spirits than she expected, well enough, in fact, to hassle Grace about her name.

Grace had long since given up trying to convince her parents to stop calling her Daisy. She was reconciled to the reality that they never would, but she did wish her mother would stop dropping hints about how much Grace's name change bothered her.

This day, with ALS hanging over them like an executioner's axe, Grace asked, as gently as she knew how, "Why does it bother you, Mother?"

Margaret furrowed her brow. "It doesn't bother me, dear. If you don't like the name you were given at birth—" she shrugged.

"You say it doesn't bother you, but it does, else you wouldn't make needly comments like that."

Margaret shook her head. "I don't know what you mean, dear."

Grace did not push back. She knew it would do no good. Her mother was a lady, in the Southernest sense of the word, even though she hadn't lived in the South since her wedding. If she said it did not bother her, she wouldn't admit even on her deathbed that it did. Grace, being Grace, smiled and changed the subject.

As she drove home that evening, the conversation with her mother rose up in her, along with the old aching wish that her mother would understand. It had been nearly 25 years—well over half of Grace's life—and still her mother did not even try to see it from Grace's perspective. When Grace thought, not for the first time, of all the things she could have changed—her morality, her religion, even her gender, for heaven's sake—and hadn't, she thought her mother very small for continuing to mind her name change. But something about it rankled, clearly, and Grace wanted things to be right between them.

Margaret deteriorated rapidly, more rapidly than anyone expected, so rapidly that Grace had little time to think about how to make things right. She was too busy caring for her mother, comforting her father, protecting her children. Two months after her diagnosis, Margaret was put on hospice. Grace's brother and sister, their spouses, and their children joined Grace at their parents' home and held vigil together. Eight days later, Margaret fell asleep and never woke up.

Grace mourned quietly, privately. Ronald alone saw her grief, her regret. With her father and brother and sister and their families, she was calm and capable and competent as ever, arranging for the funeral, the burial, the obituary, all the many details that grieving people must endure to lay their loved ones to rest. If her voice cracked or her eyes grew teary, it was only to be expected, and only for a moment.

Two months after Margaret's death, Grace made a trip to the courthouse. Then she made a trip to the cemetery. It was her 43rd birthday. She parked her old Mercedes, put on her coat, for though it was May, it was chilly, and stepped into the brisk air. Sunlight glinted across the wet grass as she made her way to her mother's plot. Standing above it, she felt too tall, so she squatted on her haunches. Grace never squatted—it was a most inelegant position—but the grass was too wet to kneel on, and

71

she felt awkward standing almost six feet above her mother's resting place.

So she squatted.

"Mother," she said. "I have something to show you." She rested her handbag on her knees and pulled out her wallet. She opened her wallet and pulled out a little piece of paper the size of a business card. "I wanted you to see this. I wanted to tell you I understand now. You thought I was rejecting you. But it was never Margaret that I minded. It was Daisy. So I put the Margaret back in. I even put it first, because it was the first name I ever had."

She turned the card over so that it faced her mother's headstone. "It says, 'Margaret Grace Kelly'. But I'm not Margaret anymore, Mother. I never was. I'm Grace. I've worn that name for so long that it's become me—or I've become it, I'm not sure which. But I wanted you to know that I hadn't let go of you by becoming me."

Grace squatted a moment longer, holding the card out so her mother could see. Then she turned it toward herself and read the name silently. She put the card in her wallet and her wallet in her handbag. Then she stood up. She looked down at her mother's grave, and behind her sunglasses, she blinked away tears. Then she turned and walked through the wet grass and the sunlight back to her waiting car.

# Reflections

Scott Delos stood in his living room, his bare feet cold on the pine floor, and stared dismally out the window into the bleak gray light of a mid-March morning. The light from the lamp behind him cast its reflection onto the window, and reflected him, too. He watched himself raise the black coffee mug to his lips, saw the bob of his Adam's apple as he swallowed. Then his gaze slipped through the sheer reflection and into the little walled garden beyond.

Already Margaret was outside, attired in her dingy raincoat and mud-caked wellies, digging in the dirt, planting some kind of flower. Flowers were Margaret's solution to everything. Flowers, soup, and bread. Illness in the family? She brought flowers, soup, and bread. New baby? Flowers, soup, and bread. Death of a loved one? Flowers, soup, and bread. She'd begun digging holes almost the moment they'd moved here last fall. And they'd eaten soup and bread every night for three months.

He took another swallow of coffee, and his gaze shifted again, catching once more on the reflection of his own face in the window. He looked haggard, exhausted. It didn't seem to matter how much sleep he got. He always woke up tired.

Sometimes he wished he wouldn't wake up at all. But the thought of death was unbearable right now, even more unbearable than the thought of life. At least in life he had hope that he might someday rebuild his ministry, reestablish his good name. If he were to die now, the only thing people would remember about him were the scandals that had erupted and ruined him. No one would remember his masterful preaching, his vast knowledge of the Scriptures, or his unique ability to make theological truths come alive.

Though he continued to stare out the window, he no longer saw Margaret or his own reflection. The coffee grew cold in his mug as images flicked across the screen of his mind—the way he'd held captive audiences of thousands by the mere modulation of his voice, the way he'd had them eating out of his hand, longing for more, more of his words, more of his wisdom, more of the truth he spoke so well. That was what staggered him, what kept him lying awake night after night: he'd spoken truth, he'd pointed to God with his words, he'd honed his native abilities to make God's name known, and God had let this happen.

There was no truth to the allegations that had ruined him. Not a shred of evidence to give credence to that woman's claims, nor a misplaced penny to wonder about. But people were fickle. Despite the packed stadiums, the standing-room-only events when people queued round the block to hear him preach, they didn't really care about truth, not when a scandal titillated their depraved sensibilities. Scott Delos the womanizing embezzler made a much more interesting story than Scott Delos the faithful husband and faithful steward. They lapped up the lies of the press as greedily as they'd lapped up the truth of his teaching.

He despised them. He despised their fair-weather faithfulness, their eager gullibility, their ingrate betrayal.

He'd spent his whole adult life telling them about God's love, God's faithfulness, God's goodness, setting them free from their bondage to fear and sin, and this is how they repaid him, by believing slander and scandal, by repeating it, by dragging his name through the dirt.

*And You!* he thought. *I gave my life for You, and what do I have to show for it? A ruined name, a ruined life.*

❦

Margaret sat back on her heels and lifted her head to the sky. A fine rain was falling, almost a mist. She felt it settle onto her face, like a caress, and watched as it condensed like silver beads on an ancient cherry tree in the neighbor's yard, whose branches overhung the wall. She had always loved this garden. Some of her happiest memories were of helping her grandmother as she pottered about tending her plants. It had grieved her deeply when Grandmother could no longer care for the little cottage.

Margaret would gladly have moved back home to take care of Grandmother so she could die in the place she had lived so long, or brought Grandmother to live with her and Scott, but Scott—well, it was no good thinking about it. She had won the argument about the cottage, at least, and it had been rented rather than sold. And she had found a good care facility only a few miles from her and Scott's house, so she was able to visit Grandmother almost every day until she died two years ago. It had brought Margaret such joy to bring flowers each week, so Grandmother could see what was in bloom, since she so seldom got to spend time out of doors.

And who would have thought that she and Scott would end up here in Grandmother's house? That she, Margaret, would be caring for the very earth that Grandmother had for so many decades tended with such love?

She smiled happily at the thought as she turned her eyes back to the earth and the primroses she was transplanting. It felt disloyal to be so glad when Scott was so miserable, but Margaret couldn't help it. These brick walls surrounding the garden and the house were a gift, shutting out the unkindness of the world, sheltering the beauty that Grandmother had spent her life cultivating. She had always found them a sort of shield, strong arms that held and protected her, and she came here as often as she could both as a child and as a grown woman, especially when Scott's ministry had taken off like a jet plane.

She'd been proud of him, and glad for him, and she'd smiled and posed, but she did not care to travel and sit for photographs and interviews as the famous preacher's wife, for she was not photogenic and even to her own eyes, she always seemed to fade into the background, no matter what the background was. It was as if she were perennially washed out, pale to the point of invisibility. That had been Scott's life, Scott's dream. She wanted dirt under her fingernails and flowers in her hair.

And now she had them. She could scarcely believe it, and dug her fingers into the cold wet earth just to feel the reality of it, the miracle. Grandmother was in Heaven, and she and Scott were here, and spring was coming. Already the daffodils had begun to bloom, and her pansies and primroses were ready for planting out. Impulsively, she grabbed her clippers, snipped a daffodil stem, and tucked it behind her ear. Though she knew her hood would probably squash it, she smiled anyway.

As she stood to move a few feet away to plant another primrose, she caught sight of Scott standing in the window. She turned her smile on him and lifted her hand in a small wave, but he did not respond. Her shoulders drooped a bit as she squatted down to transplant the next primrose along the border. Poor Scott. He was so unhappy, so eaten up with bitterness over all that had happened. She worked her spade into the soil. He could only see that he was no longer useful and necessary and loved by large numbers of people. He had no thought, or did not care, that he could be useful and necessary to her, and that she loved him still. In some ways she loved him now more than ever.

With a deft, gentle twist, she pried the primrose out of its tiny terra cotta pot and slid it into the hole she'd dug. She would have been delighted to have Scott join her here in the garden. He needn't dig in the dirt if he didn't want to, and she knew he wouldn't, but he could sit on the little patio and read if he liked, or talk with her. But he never talked to her anymore, not really. He lived isolated in his own mind, staring out the window and seeing nothing, or sitting in his dark office staring at the computer screen. She knew he sometimes watched old YouTube videos of himself preaching, as if to reassure himself that all he had lost had been real. She filled around the little transplant with soil, gently tamped it down with her fingers, and looked back at the window, where Scott still stood, his coffee mug in his hand and his eyes unseeing. Her heart ached. He was fading into a shadow of himself. His eyes looked sunken in his face, and his skin hung on him like clothes two sizes too large. He hardly ate and he hardly slept.

Standing up, she moved again, closer to the window where he stood, but he did not see her. She squatted back down and began to dig another hole when a sudden motion in the tail of her eye attracted her attention. A squirrel had leapt from the top of the wall to a branch of the cherry tree and was running along it, scattering water drops like a bag of pearls bursting all over the dormant hollyhocks along the east wall. Another wild leap and he was in the old apple tree that spread its arms over the south-east corner of the garden, careering madly along its branches until he disappeared with a final flying leap over the back wall. Laughing, Margaret turned to look at Scott, hoping he had seen it, hoping he would smile at her. He hadn't, and he didn't. She returned to her primroses.

❦

"Scott?"

Through the headphones, Margaret's voice barely registered above the charismatic voice of the preacher on the stage. Scott ignored her and kept watching the mesmerizing man on the screen. It was hard to believe it was himself he was seeing. It was hard to believe how good he had been. Every day that is what he thought: he had been really, really good.

"Scott?"

Her voice was louder now, and he could hear a tap-tap on the door.

"I'm busy," he called in a voice he hardly recognized.

She tapped again.

He ripped off the headphones. "What?" he barked.

A moment's pause, then, "It's lunchtime. I made soup. I thought since it's stopped raining that we might eat outside?"

He groaned. Of course she'd made soup. He was sick of soup. And he hated that garden, the way the walls seemed to close him in and cut him off from the world. He settled the headphones back over his ears. "No, thanks," he called. "I'm not hungry." He backed up the video to the place he'd left off when Margaret had interrupted him.

The door opened behind him, and Margaret stepped inside the dark room. The light from the hall hit the screen in front of him, superimposing Margaret's silhouette over the image of the preacher. He whipped off the headphones yet again, fumbled with his mouse to shut the browser window, and whirled around in his chair. "I said I wasn't hungry!"

She gave him a timid smile. "I know, but I'd already made it, and you need to eat. You're getting awfully thin, you know." She set a tray on his desk in front of the monitor. On it were a bowl of soup—he couldn't tell what kind in the light from the screen—a plate with three pieces of buttered bread, and a mug of either tea or coffee—again he couldn't tell which. He waited, but Margaret didn't leave. Instead she looked around the room, taking in the bare walls, the closed blinds, the blank Word document on the screen, and finally himself. He could not bear the steadiness of her gray eyes on him, and looked away.

She swallowed audibly and said, "I think you should come outside."

"I—can't." And he couldn't. That garden seemed symbolic of his shrunken, isolated life. He almost shuddered. "I'm busy."

"Yes, I can see that." She looked meaningfully at the blank document on the screen. Then she turned and left the room, not quite closing the door behind her.

He sat huddled in his chair for a moment, feeling wretched and defeated. Slowly he reached for the mug and took a sip. Tea. Very strong. And hot. It warmed him. He took another sip. And another, and he realized that despite what he'd told Margaret, he was quite hungry. He pulled the tray of food away from the monitor, dipped the bread in the soup, and took a bite. The bread was tangy. Sourdough probably. Had Margaret made it?

Another tap on the door.

"Yes?" he called around the mouthful of soup and bread.

The door to the hall opened again, and again Margaret entered. This time he turned his head to look at her.

"Since you're too busy to come outside," she said, "I brought outside to you." She set a jug of daffodils on the desk, kissed the top of his head, and slipped back out of the room, leaving the door open behind her. Light from the hall spilled onto his desk, illuminating the golden faces of the daffodils.

# Crossword

She was the last in line to board the train in Seattle that afternoon, and I saw—you couldn't help seeing—that her face was pale, her eyes were bloodshot, and the hand that held her purse trembled.

"Room number, ma'am?" I asked.

"Oh," she said, so softly I could barely hear her. "I'm sorry, sir. I don't know."

"Reservation number?"

"Oh." She fumbled in her purse. "Hold on."

"Last name?"

"Here it is." She pulled out her phone.

"Last name?" I repeated.

"O'Connor. But here's my reservation number." She held her phone's screen toward me.

I glanced at her phone, then at my list. "Room 24. To the right, up the stairs, then to the left. I'll be up shortly with your dinner reservation."

When I reached her room twenty minutes later, she sat ramrod straight in her seat, staring out the window with red eyes.

"I took the liberty," I said, "of making your dinner reservation at 5:00."

"Oh." She looked down at her lap and glanced at the watch on her wrist. "But that's right now."

"Yes."

"Oh!" Her gaze flicked in my direction and then fastened on the floor near my feet. "I—could I—is there any way I could eat in my room?"

I pursed my lips and withdrew.

In the dining car, which reeked of hot oil and fish, the cook slammed an oven shut. She was run off her feet, she said, booked till closing, and no, she didn't have time to box up a meal, not till after the dining room closed at eight, and maybe not then. Room 24 could come eat now, she said, or wait indefinitely. Her call.

Back at Room 24, I explained the options.

"I think I'd rather wait," she said. Her face was very white except for dark areas under her red-rimmed eyes. She sat upright with her hands clasped tightly in her lap.

"Very well," I said, and placed a menu on the tray table beside her. "I will bring you dinner at eight, when I go get my own."

"Oh, you don't have to do that," she said in a rush. "I can go get it. You don't have to wait on me."

"Yes, I do. Unless you eat in the dining car. Railway regulations."

"Oh." She unclasped and reclasped her hands.

I waited.

After a long moment she said quietly, "Yes, I think I would prefer to eat later."

"Fine."

An hour past Everett we spent 45 minutes sitting on a siding. Brian, the conductor, passed me in the corridor. "Freight train," he muttered.

I nodded and scowled. Service continued whether we sat on a siding or rolled forward on time. Waiting here just meant we had to serve the passengers for that much longer. And put up with their complaints. I continued on down the hall.

It was past eight when I arrived at Room 24 with her dinner—salad, entrée, and silverware—which I set on the tray table. She'd been on the train more than three hours and so far as I could see had neither eaten nor drunk anything, had hardly moved—but she didn't reach for the food, only thanked me and continued staring out the window, very fixedly. It was growing dusky.

Suddenly, the light outside went dark as though someone had flicked a switch—we had entered the train tunnel through the Cascades—but she seemed not to notice that the passing scenery was gone. I clamped my jaw shut, inhaled through my nose, and left her to stare at the darkness outside the window.

I took my own meal to the crew lounge, where Brian sat at a table, working a crossword. His bald head, concentrated expression, and the tapping of his pencil were clearly reflected in the window of the train. I slid into the seat across from him and began to eat.

"Perfect timing, Jimmy. I'm stuck. Four letter word for 'keen,'" he said. "Second letter's an E."

"Weep."

"Ah, that kind of keen." He wrote it in.

I took two bites. From the corner of my eye, I caught the movement of my own reflection in the window as I moved the fork from the plate to my mouth.

"Five letter word for 'peer,'" Brian said. "I thought maybe 'stare,' but the last letter's an L."

"Equal. Or coeval."

"Coeval? What kind of word is that?"

"Doesn't matter," I said. "It's six letters anyway."

He shrugged as he spelled *equal* under his breath and wrote it in.

I took two more bites.

"Seven, no, eight letter word for 'long-suffering.' What the devil is long-suffering? Third letter's a T, last letter's an E."

"Patience."

He frowned but wrote it in. "How come you always know these, Jimmy? You're a machine. Never miss a beat."

I shrugged and kept eating.

"All right, smart guy, what about this? 'Dessert in Paris.' Eight, nine, ten, eleven letters."

"You got any?"

"Only E."

"Beginning, middle, or end?"

"All three. Third letter, fifth letter, and last letter."

I took another bite. "Crème brulée."

"How d'you spell that?"

I told him.

"Dang, Jimmy," he said with a laugh. "It just fits." He worked in silence until I took the last bite of my dinner. "Done," he said and put down his pencil. "Crème brulée!" he said with another short laugh just as the train emerged from the tunnel. Dusky light filled the crew lounge, muting our reflections in the window. "That broke it open, Jimmy. Thanks." I nodded, gathered my dishes and utensils, and left.

I dropped my tray in the dining car and then stopped by Room 24.

The door was closed. I knocked.

"Come in."

I found her in exactly the position I had left her, staring still, unmoving, out the window. There was nothing to see except silhouettes, a repeated flickering of dark sky and darker trees. The light from the corridor showed her reflection pale in the window. The meal I'd brought was on the tray, untouched.

She looked away from the window to gaze at the food in front of her. "I haven't eaten any dinner yet." She said it like she was just now realizing it.

"You might want to," I said. "It isn't getting any warmer."

She nodded.

"On second thought, you might want to eat this first." I held out the ice cream sandwich I'd snagged from the galley. "Otherwise it'll melt."

"Oh," she said, taking the sandwich. She looked at me, and a small smile softened her face. "That's kind of you."

# Primroses for Nell Parker

*For Wendell Berry, with great admiration:*
*Imitation is, after all, the sincerest form of flattery.*

Nell Parker woke with a headache. She could hear rain pelting the windows as she lay staring into the cold dark and wishing she could fall back asleep. When Alan's alarm went off, she closed her eyes and pretended to be sleeping. She did not want him to know she was unwell. He went into the bathroom to take a shower, and she lay in bed, wondering if it would be better to lie still or get up. Alan dressed and went out to the kitchen to make coffee and toast.

She sat up in bed and felt tempted to lie back down again and pull the covers over her aching head. The air was cold; they could not afford to run the heater at night, and it was an old heater anyway; it took its sweet time warming the rectory each morning. She got up, slid her feet into her slippers, pulled on a thick wool sweater over her pajama shirt, went into the bathroom, and took an ibuprofen. Her face in the mirror looked pale. She pinched her cheeks, ran her hands through her hair, and wished she hadn't. The pain in her head beat a little staccato against the inside of her skull. She turned off the light and went to the kitchen.

Alan handed her a cup of coffee, steaming in the cold air of the rectory, and a plate of toast with jam.

"Good morning!" he said with a smile that she managed to return, though she feared it looked more like a grimace.

"You okay?" he asked with concern.

She nodded, not looking at him, and held the coffee cup close to her lips.

He ate two pieces of toast with peanut butter and another two with jam. Ordinarily, she'd have sat across from him and watched him eat—his long-fingered hands were beautifully expressive, and he clearly delighted in the taste of even simple fare—but this morning she turned to stare out the kitchen window at the gray sky and the falling rain. Wind lashed the cedars in the lot across the street. She did not eat the toast he'd made for her.

"Not hungry?" he asked.

She shook her head, and pain stabbed through her left eye.

He poured another cup of coffee, stirred milk into it—they could not afford cream, or even half-and-half—and eyed her toast.

"You're welcome to it," she said. "I'll eat something later."

He bit into the toast, and the crunch of it almost made her wince. She looked back out the window and clutched the coffee cup for warmth, wishing he would go.

He lingered, sipping slowly. Coffee was one of his pleasures, and he relished it, especially on a cold gray morning. He was not one to sit and savor, preferring to be up and about, working, planning, helping, getting things done, moving things forward.

This moment in the morning when he sat and sipped his coffee was, usually, one of her favorites of the day. He was, for a few minutes, still and present, quiet in his enjoyment. For Nell, it was an anchor of her day, reminding her why she had married him.

She loved his forward-leaning momentum, the way even in his stillness he seemed to be moving. He was like a river, she thought, always moving and yet always himself. When the alarm went off in the morning, he rolled from bed and stepped straight into the flow of the day's work. Its momentum carried him even now, in this moment of quiet enjoyment. The little small-town parish that he pastored afforded him both too many and too few opportunities: too many because there was always more work to be done than he could do himself—the building was large, and old, and in constant need of repair—and too few because the congregation had dwindled so dramatically during the pandemic that there were now only a handful of parishioners. The pandemic had been hard on everyone, but even though their income had plummeted, he and Nell were not going to starve, or freeze, and week after week, Alan preached his homilies and served the Eucharist, and somehow it was enough.

But he knew her love of beauty, and she realized that part of his forward movement, in the months since they married, stemmed from his desire to surround her with beautiful things that gave her pleasure. It was his desire more than hers, and she teased him about it. There was a silver lining in her having sold just six paintings in sixteen months, she said; it kept the walls of the rectory graced with art. And Alan was a musician; his fiddle, banjo, and guitar hung on the wall of the living room, except when he pulled them down to play of an evening. "And certain kinds of pleasure are free," she added with a saucy smile as she leaned over to kiss him. Still, the church could pay only a pittance, so when he wasn't working at the church or making a pastoral call, he worked for his brother-in-law.

This morning, delaying the writing of his homily, he was going to help Kevin install sheetrock at the house whose kitchen he was remodeling. She thought of him and Kevin meeting at the house, hefting the sheetrock out of Kevin's truck and into the garage, and the two of them hefting it again, one of them holding it in place on the wall while the other shot the nail gun, the sound exploding—bam!bam!bam!bam!—shaking the house and rattling the windows.

Alan pushed his chair back from the table and stood. He set his cup and plate in the sink. She set her mug down on the table and went to him, resting her head on his shoulder for a moment as he wrapped his arms around her. "It's dismal out there," he said. "Stay inside, okay?"

She nodded her head against his shoulder and wished he did not have to go, wished she could stay here in the circle of his arms. She stepped back. "Have you got your tools?"

"By the door." He had gathered last night what he would need today. He put on his heavy work coat, a hand-me-down from Kevin; his woolen cap that she'd found for a dollar at the thrift store; and his gloves, a Christmas present from his parents. He picked up his toolbox, started out the back door, and then turned around. "Don't worry about going over to the church. I'll take care of it when I get home."

"Okay," she said.

He shut the door. And now the kitchen was an empty cell of glaring lamplight that reflected off the windows, which were gray and clattering in the wind and streaked with the rain that beat upon them. She switched off the overhead light and closed her eyes for a moment, wondering when the ibuprofen would kick in. Then she went to the sink and dumped her lukewarm coffee down the drain. She washed the mugs and plates and put them away. The kitchen contained a table and four chairs, only two of them matching. A small counter ran under the east-facing window, with cabinets below and open shelves flanking the window on either side. The refrigerator, its door handle duct-taped together, sat against the north wall; the stove and oven against the south, with the range hood hanging from the ceiling above. The stove was old, the color of putty, and finicky. It and the refrigerator had been here when Alan moved into the rectory six years ago.

She heard his truck pull out of the carport, heading into the alley behind the church. She wiped down the table and leaned heavily against it for a moment. She stared unseeing at the badly scuffed floorboards. Gradually her eyes focused and she realized there were crumbs on the floor, and dirt. There always seemed to be crumbs and dirt, no matter how often she swept. Perhaps the floor, being so old and badly used, took its revenge by spitting crumbs and dirt up from its depths. She took the broom from the laundry alcove beside the back door and swept the kitchen. Then she swept the other rooms as well. The rectory had only four: the kitchen, the living room, the bedroom, and a bathroom. It was old and poorly built and had been used as a storeroom for over a decade before Alan moved in.

The living room wallpaper, Nell guessed, had been put up in the 50's. Probably its ropes of flowers had been quietly colorful then, but now it was faded to varying shades of gray. Nell wanted to take it down, but didn't dare, for fear the plaster behind it would crumble away. The fir floors were worn to white near the doorways and around the stove and before the sink in the kitchen. Around the old clawfoot tub in the bathroom, the floor was warped. To keep them from stubbing their toes on its uneven surface, Nell had put down the biggest bathmat she could find.

Though the house was dark and drafty, she tried to make it homey. She had made curtains—there had been none in the house when she moved in; Alan had simply tacked an old bed sheet over the window in the bedroom. The curtains were a cheerful calico print, white and yellow flowers on a sky-blue background, a bolt of which she'd found on clearance at the fabric store. She made skirts of the same cloth for the square plastic totes she'd had since college, which served as nightstands and in which they stored their extra sheets and blankets. She'd also made a matching bed skirt to hide the boxes they kept under the bed; the rectory had no closets. She covered the faded wallpaper with portraits of saints she had painted. They looked down from their canvases like a benevolent cloud of witnesses, cheering her on. Usually they felt like company and helped her feel less alone. But not today.

Every motion she made sent little sparks of light dancing before her eyes. She felt light-headed and yet heavy, as though she were moving through water. After she put the broom away, she let herself sink down into one of the wooden chairs at the table, and she rested her head on her arms.

It was unlike her to be ill—she had sailed through the pandemic without so much as a cold or a sore throat—and it was unlike her to sit with her head in her arms when there was work to be done. She wondered if she'd finally succumbed to Covid, and she remembered that she had been annoyed with Alan last night; about what she could not recall; perhaps it had something to do with his working with Kevin today; or perhaps not. She couldn't remember. Her head ached, scattering her thoughts like the drops of rain spitting on the windows.

And then she remembered her long, irritated silence, the heaviness of it, the way it weighted the air like water, and how she had felt she was drowning in it. She remembered the way Alan seemed not to notice that anything was wrong, the way he'd kissed her, told her he loved her, walked into the bedroom, and gone to bed. He had been asleep when she came in and crawled under the covers beside him.

And then she remembered that the vestry was meeting at the church tonight. Which meant she needed to go next-door and clean the bathrooms, and vacuum, and make sure the kitchen was clean, too. Perhaps that was why she'd been annoyed with Alan last night—because he wouldn't be here to help her. This was not what she'd signed up for. Being a pastor's wife was one thing. Being expected to clean the church bathrooms was another.

She and Alan had married a year and a half earlier, in the first summer of the pandemic, when she was 37 and he was 41. She had never met anybody like him, and she had begun to despair that she ever would. He had a warm smile, an infectious laugh, and a disarming ability to listen well, as if the forward movement of his being paused a moment out of the main current, stilling like a deep pool and waiting quietly while you talked, waiting till you were done, before moving slowly back out into the rush of the river, taking you with him.

That was how it had been. He had listened to her, taken her seriously, and on her own terms, and when he returned to his forward-facing ways, she had found she wanted to go with him. Besides, he made her laugh, laugh till she cried, both of them weak with laughter over the silliest things. He delighted in the smallest details, found humor everywhere, made their poor life rich with the readiness of his laughter, the wideness of his conversation, the clarity of his vision.

He had been in business for ten years after college when he had quit and gone back to school, to seminary. And then he had been ordained. After three years as an assistant rector in a city church, his sister had called him and begged him to apply for the position at St. Brigid's. "There's scope for you, here, Alan," Min had said. "We're wounded and bleeding, and we need someone with a big heart and a long view." And so he had left the city and come here, to a parish that had been shrinking for a decade, shrinking in size and shrinking in soul.

By the time Nell arrived in January of 2020, Alan had worked a seeming miracle. He had focused on shepherding his little flock of 23 people, on helping them process the pain they had been through, the betrayal and the abuse, on helping them heal and forgive. And the church had begun to grow again. New families trickled in. Single people in their 20's and 30's. College students. Retirees. Alan led them back again and again to the Good Shepherd, the Crucified One, the Resurrected Lord, so when Min had seen Nell's triptych of the life of Jesus at the college chapel in the fall of 2019, she told Alan, "We need her to paint something for us." And then she and Kevin donated the funds.

"I want the Good Shepherd, the Crucifixion, and the Resurrection," Min told Nell, and showed her the space where the triptych would be displayed, on the blank wall behind the altar.

Nell had blanched. She did not work in large scale. Her pieces were small, simple, intimate. She had never done anything on a large scale, much less a scale as large as this. She almost said no. Then Alan had come and listened to her, and he brainstormed ways Nell's small pieces might work in the larger space of the sanctuary until he hit on an idea she thought was workable: she would paint the triptych on the front of the altar.

And then the pandemic hit. The church closed indefinitely. Alan figured out how to livestream a Eucharist service. Nell continued painting. They were frequently in the same space, she painting, he fiddling with iPhones and tripods and computers. They wore masks and they worked mostly in silence, but every day he offered her a cup of coffee, and brought it to her in a ceramic mug. Alan abominated Styrofoam and paper. "Ruins the taste of the coffee." Spaced several pews apart, they would talk as they sipped their coffee. He asked intelligent questions about her painting and listened as she answered at length. They talked of theology and books, art and music, their work and their travels, and the connection between them strengthened and deepened, perhaps accelerated by the fact that they both lived alone, and the world was in shut-down, and everyone was keeping indoors and away from others.

They were married in July, at his parents' farm in the Skagit Valley, under an arbor of roses, with only his parents and Min, Kevin, and their three children in attendance.

Nell's mother had not approved of her becoming a painter, much less a painter of religious works, and she was annoyed but not surprised that Nell was marrying a priest. She could have driven up from Oregon—Nell asked her to—but she declined; the pandemic made traveling too risky, she said. But Nell knew her mother would have found some other reason not to come had there not been a pandemic. At least this excuse had some validity.

Nell's sister lived in New York. She was a financial analyst or something like that. Nell never quite understood exactly what it was that Cass did for a living. Cass had never cared about Nell's work, either. Art was a good way to starve, she said, and though she never said as much, she clearly thought that people who wanted to starve had better do it and let everyone else get on with their lives. When Nell called to tell her about Alan, Cass's only response had been, "I thought it was illegal to marry a priest," and then she'd begun detailing the woes of living in Manhattan during a pandemic. "I haven't been outside in four months. Four. Months." She got all her food delivered, whether groceries or take-out, and sat staring at a screen all day. "I'm going to end up in a lunatic asylum, I just know it."

"You could come out for the wedding," Nell said. "Change of scene."

Cass laughed. "If I'm going to get on an airplane and risk my life breathing other people's germs, I want to do it going someplace warm and tropical."

Nell wondered why she kept trying to reach out to her mother and sister, even as she knew she always would.

Alan had been living in the rectory for five years when he and Nell married, and it was definitely bachelor's quarters. Min had organized a cleaning crew, and the women of the church came one by one to scour the place from top to bottom before Nell moved in. She brought with her little beyond her paints and canvases, only the kitchen table and chairs (which replaced the card table Alan had been using), an antique pine sideboard that sat in the living room opposite the fireplace, the sofa she had bought at a used furniture store when she returned from

Hungary in 2010, and an antique pine armoire that took up half of one wall of their tiny bedroom. She had never had much money, and now she had less: her adjunct teaching job was not renewed because of the pandemic, and churches everywhere were hurting for money; most of them did not see the need for sacred art in their sanctuaries at the best of times, and these were not the best of times. She opened an Etsy shop and made a few dollars selling cards and prints.

Nell had moved into the rectory the same month the doors of the church re-opened. It was a different world, this small-town parish in which she found herself. The pandemic had undone all of Alan's work of the previous five years; there were no longer even 23 people in attendance. The parish was down to five couples, and two widows. But Nell could not grieve over small numbers, for those twelve souls created for her a world of warmth and community, made all the warmer by the coldness of the pandemic.

Except for Alan and herself, Min and Kevin were the youngest, and the only family with young children. Jake and Barbara Johnson were in their 80's and had been at St. Brigid's since 1957. Their son Gerald had been at St. Brigid's his entire life; he and his wife, Gladys, had been empty-nesters, but their two college-age children were then at home, their schools having shut down for the foreseeable future. Henry and Joyce Garland were also in their 80's, Mike and Sherry Raymond were in their 70's, and Jennie O'Dell was in her 60's; she was head of the altar guild and kept the church in fresh flowers. Tess Zimmerman was only a few years older than Min, and worked as a nurse; her husband had died of cancer two years before. Nell loved them all. They had lived and worshiped and eaten and wept and rejoiced together, weathering difficulty and offering solace, steadfastly remaining at St. Brigid's, investing their lives in one another and this church.

It seemed strange and wonderful to her that in 2020, there was still a place where the ties of relationship went back decades, where people were devoted to the care and keeping of a church, of a community and a place. She was used to city life with its constantly shifting population, where money was the medium of exchange and people shopped for churches the way they shopped for clothes. But these old souls would never dream of leaving St. Brigid's. It was their church, almost their home. They had lived and worked alongside one another for so long that they seemed to belong to one another, and to the church. They were the church.

Kevin and Min were the newcomers, having been at St. Brigid's for a mere 14 years, but they were both so capable and adaptable and so glad to pitch in that they had woven themselves right into the fabric of the community. Kevin was the senior warden; as a contractor, he was adept at knowing what needed to be done to keep their old building from crumbling down on their heads. Cost was always an issue, but they did as much of the work themselves as they could. The summer Nell married Alan, they all pitched in and painted the outside of the building. "Many hands make light work," Henry Garland had said, though his hands were so blighted by arthritis that he could hardly use them anymore. Still, he had ferried ice-cold drinks to the painters as they sweated in the sun, laughing and joking, and despite the mask over his nose and mouth, they all knew from the crinkles at the corners of his eyes that he was smiling at them.

Nell loved each of them individually and all of them together. She tried not to have favorites, but she couldn't help loving Jennie O'Dell best of all. Jennie was a rosy, smiling woman, round and glad and good and green-thumbed. She kept a large and beautiful cutting garden, and each week she brought vases full of flowers to set beside the pulpit. She was a genius at making bouquets. Even in winter she managed to bring something to brighten the sanctuary, perhaps a bough of winter-fire dogwood or a small vase with a half-dozen snowdrops that she set on the lectern. She regularly brought a vase of flowers to the rectory, and if Nell was home, she was usually able to persuade Jennie to come in for tea. "My children won't like it," Jennie would say. "They're worried. They won't even come visit. Do you know, I haven't hugged my grandchildren in six months! Just seen them on a screen." Then she'd smile and wink at Nell. "But I'm 67 years old—old enough to have a cup of tea, don't you think?" Nell would smile and hold open the door for her.

As head of the altar guild, Jennie trained Nell in the liturgies of preparing the altar, of washing the cloths, of cleaning the candlesticks. Every woman in the church knew how to lay the table and could be trusted to take the altar cloths home to launder. It was important to Jennie that Nell know how, too. And so she learned.

The other women invited Nell over for lunch or tea. She went to each house separately, for they were all being careful, out of love for one another, to keep gatherings to two or at most three people. They came together, masked, for Sunday Eucharist, each couple sitting in their own pew, all spaced several pews apart. It was a cavernous old church, and their presence in it, all separated like that, felt to Nell like they were so many pebbles scattered across a wide swath of sand. She wished they could gather near the altar rail and hear one another sing. The women praised Nell's paintings that now graced the front of the altar.

Beautiful, said Joyce. Wonderful, said Barbara. They help me listen to the homily, said Jennie. Or if they don't, added Gladys, they certainly help me think about Jesus.

In the early summer of 2021, after everyone was vaccinated and the mask mandate had been lifted, the women gathered in the parish hall and peeled off the old wallpaper and scraped off the glue. Nell, Min, and Tess, as the youngest, climbed ladders to get to the wallpaper near the ceiling. It was the first time they'd all been together, unmasked, since Nell had known them. They laughed and chatted and threw wallpaper glue at one another and generally behaved like schoolgirls on summer break.

In August, when they were told they had to put their masks back on, Tess had still organized the women's annual outing to a blueberry farm in Skagit Valley. Barbara and Joyce picked a few berries, but they spent most of the day sitting in camp chairs under a large sun umbrella that Min had brought, telling stories to Min's children who had quickly tired of picking berries. The other women would traipse over with a full bucket of blueberries and set it at Barbara and Joyce's feet, like a votive offering.

They picked over 200 pounds of berries that day. Nell, who knew nothing of canning, spent the rest of the week in the church kitchen, where Gladys, Sherry, and Jennie taught her how to make blueberry jam and blueberry butter and blueberry syrup, how to sterilize the jars and the lids. They chatted and laughed as they worked, and later Nell felt teary as she remembered all the ways these women had welcomed her this past year, enfolded her into themselves, sharing their knowledge with her, making her one of them. They sorted the jars into eight boxes, but not evenly. Min got the most, "because she has five mouths to feed," Jennie explained, and Gladys got the next most because her son was home from college, and Nell got the next most for reasons that made no sense; she suspected it was simply because Alan was the rector, and she tried to argue, but she did not win. All fall and winter, she felt a sense of gratitude and glad satisfaction when she saw those rows of jars sitting on the shelf beside her kitchen window.

❧

She looked up at the jars now, but she felt nothing except cold and tired. She needed to go to the church. If she waited, she might not go at all. Shoving herself to her feet, she walked wearily to the bedroom. The bedcovers lay open and inviting. She ignored them and went into the bathroom to take a Covid test. While she waited for the results, she slipped, shivering, out of her pajamas and into jeans and a long-sleeved t-shirt. She pulled the wool sweater back over her head, tied her hair in a knot, and put on a beanie. She made the bed and sat on it, slumped over, staring at the wall without seeing it. When the timer on her phone went off, she checked the Covid test. Negative. She'd half hoped it would be positive, so she would not have to go to the church. Sighing, she pulled on her shoes and headed to the front door, where she slipped into her rain jacket and out the door.

Yesterday had been sunny, with puffy white clouds floating in a sea of blue sky. There were buds on the cherry trees in the church yard, and yellow crocuses had sprouted along the east side of the rectory, in the little strip of lawn that separated the house from the carport and alley. But in the night, the wind had risen and driven rain clouds in from the Sound. The cherry trees in the church yard tossed their branches as the wind whipped through them, and the brave little crocuses bent their yellow heads toward the ground. As Nell stepped off the porch, a gust of wind hit her square in the chest, slicing right through her jacket and sweater. The rain, driven sideways by the wind, spattered into her face. She put her head down and walked quickly to the church.

By the time she let herself into the building, she was chilled to the bone and out of breath. The lights behind her eyes were spinning like tops. She sagged against the wall, waiting for her breathing to even out, the lights to stop spinning. Finally, she pushed herself upright and went to the women's bathroom where the cleaning supplies were kept. Ordinarily she could clean the bathrooms in half an hour, but she was so tired and grew so dizzy that it took her twice as long. She did not vacuum. The mere thought of the roar of the ancient Kirby made her head throb. She put away the cleaning supplies and braved the wind and the rain as she fought her way back to the rectory. Stumbling up the steps and into the house, she collapsed on the sofa. Her jacket was soaked, as were her jeans. She knew she should get up and change, but she did not want to move.

The rectory was cold. It was often cold. Mostly she did not mind bundling up in warm wool sweaters, or putting on an extra pair of socks, or wearing a scarf and beanie in the house. She and Alan made it a kind of game to see how little they could use the heater, how little money they could spend. They went without internet service, choosing to use the church's if they needed to get online. They sold Nell's car—it wasn't worth much—to save on the insurance. They ate a lot of pasta, and beans, and rice. Nell had not been much of a cook when she and Alan married. Alan knew how to make three dinners, all of them involving a whole chicken and a crock pot. Nell quickly realized that if she wanted to eat something other than chicken chili, chicken curry, or chicken stew, she was going to have to make it herself. She learned from the older women of the parish how to make pasta sauce from a can of tomatoes so that it did not taste like a can of tomatoes. She learned that onions and garlic, salt and spices, were cheap ways to make beans and rice, and pasta sauce, taste good. She learned to make do without cream in her coffee.

And yet, despite their poverty, despite the pandemic, they were not unhappy. Alan could find humor in almost anything, and they laughed often. He'd pull down his banjo and play a silly song, singing with a twang that would set her laughing till her sides ached. When he responded to something she'd said with one of Henry Garland's down-to-earth aphorisms in Henry Garland's deep bass voice—"Many hands make light work, Nell," "An ounce of prevention is worth a pound of cure, Nell," "Handsome is as handsome does, Nell,"—she couldn't help laughing. And he would show her funny videos on his phone, the two of them huddled together under a blanket on the sofa, her legs hooked over his, and even when she didn't find the videos all that funny, Alan's great shout of laughter was so contagious she would laugh anyway.

When it snowed that winter and shut the whole town down, Alan got dinner trays from the church kitchen, and the two of them used the trays to sled down the hill behind the church. It was a rather steep hill, and Nell screamed every time she went down, and then laughed at herself for screaming. They spent most of the day trudging up the hill and sliding down, joined by children of the neighborhood on real sleds and, once, by a police officer who used Alan's tray to race three kids to the bottom of the hill.

And when she sold her first painting in six months, they celebrated by building a fire in the fireplace and roasting hot dogs over it. They washed the hot dogs down with Nell's favorite hard cider.

Over the months of that first year, Nell learned to understand where she was. It took longer than it should have, thanks to the map app on her phone, which guided her effortlessly from place to place but kept her from internalizing her surroundings. Finally she put the phone away and got a physical map at the library and studied it, scribing the contours of the hills onto her mind so she could see them whenever she needed to go somewhere. St. Brigid's sat atop the south end of East Hill, its spire reaching to the sky, its front doors facing west. The rectory huddled beside it on the north side. Down the hill to the southwest lay the bay; northwest was downtown. The high school raised its brick bulk atop the north end of the hill, a mile from the rectory. If you continued down the hill in that direction, you'd reach the college and then the river, which flowed west, around the north side of Church Hill, and into the Sound.

She'd walked the streets of East Hill, north and south, east and west, until she knew where all the parks and gardens were, where the library was, and the tea shop, and the coffee shops, until she knew which were her favorite houses, her favorite streets.

And now she felt like she belonged here, not simply because she knew her way around but because she knew the people—the people in the parish all lived on the hill, and she knew her way to all their houses; she knew the shortcuts through parks and pedestrian-only trails, and she saw the same people on her walks: the tall old man with shining white hair who was always out walking his Westie whenever she visited the Garlands; the young mother with the double stroller who was often at the park on Elm Street; the elderly couple who frequented Charlotte's Gardens; the young runner whom she saw whenever she walked to the overlook across from the Gardens.

Once a month, on a night when it wasn't raining, she and Alan waited till after dark and then they walked from the rectory to the Garlands' house, where they stood outside and prayed for Henry and Joyce. Then they turned their steps to the home of the younger Johnsons, then to Jennie O'Dell's, to Min and Kevin's, to Tess Zimmerman's, to the Raymonds', and finally to the elder Johnsons. At each house they stood outside and prayed. Nell loved those nights, loved the way she and Alan traced the same route from house to house, their steps like a thread that wove all of the houses together, their prayers rising like smoke from a hearth fire, a light and a warmth that drew them into the very heart of God and one another.

But now those nights seemed far away and unimportant. She shivered in her wet clothes and closed her eyes. She felt bereft and abandoned, a feeling that used to be familiar, though she had forgotten it these past twenty months. Now it came back, like a breaker on the shore, and made her memories of community and laughter and belonging feel like so much driftwood tossed onto the sand, like pebbles sucked from their temporary homes on the beach back into the sea. The roar of waves seemed to fill her head. She was small and fragile. They were all small and fragile. Their community, their very bodies, could be so easily broken. Covid wasn't defeated. Maybe it would mutate and kill them all.

Her phone rang, a sound like church bells tolling.

Groggily, Nell pulled herself into a sitting position on the sofa. She must have fallen asleep. Where had she put her phone? She followed the sound to the bathroom and found it lying on the counter next to the Covid test. The ringing stopped. She closed her eyes. She should see who it was. She should call who-ever it was back. She did neither. Instead, she stripped off her wet jacket and jeans and left them lying on the floor. She pulled on a pair of sweatpants and crawled into bed. The phone rang again, or maybe it was the bells at the church. Was it time for Eucharist? The bells kept tolling. No, it was her phone. It was her mother, calling to tell her she'd overslept and what kind of lousy pastor's wife was she anyway? No, it was the rain, coming in through the roof, making a puddle on the bathroom floor where she'd left her jacket and jeans. She had to get up and get a bucket so the puddle didn't spread into the bedroom. She tried to open her eyes, but her eyelids were too heavy. She was going to miss Eucharist. The bedroom seemed to tilt like the steep roof of St. Brigid's, and she felt herself sliding into darkness.

ߦ

Nell woke to the smell of coffee. The rain had stopped. She opened her eyes. Watery yellow light seeped through the window and washed her in its warmth. On the fabric-covered plastic tote that served as her nightstand sat a squat terra cotta pot full of yellow primroses. Through the open door of the bedroom, she could see into the living room. Jennie O'Dell was sitting in the rocking chair beside the window, a jug of flowers at her elbow: jonquils, daffodils, hyacinth, crocus, windflower, in shades from white to sunny yellow to fuchsia to deep purple.

Jennie rocked placidly as she looked out the window and sipped her coffee. She seemed to feel Nell's eyes on her and turned her head. "You're awake," she said with a motherly smile that warmed Nell to her toes. "You want some coffee?"

Nell shook her head.

"Min called me," Jennie said, standing and coming to the door of the bedroom. "Father Alan told Kevin this morning that you weren't feeling well and shouldn't be alone and he wasn't going to be able to work because he wanted to be home with you, but Kevin needed his help, so he called Min and asked her to come check on you, but Min had to be at the college today, so she called me. And here I am."

Nell smiled, but tears started to her eyes. Alan had known. He had seen she was unwell. He had not wanted to leave her alone.

"How're you feeling now, honey?" Jennie asked.

"Better."

"You want anything?"

"No," Nell said. She didn't need anything. Her head had stopped aching. She was warm and cozy. She was seen and loved. "Thank you for the flowers."

"They're pretty, aren't they?" Jennie nodded toward the pot on Nell's nightstand. "I thought you might like something to brighten your room."

"I did," Nell said. "I do." She smiled, closed her eyes, and fell back asleep.

# Acknowledgements

Many thanks to Jody Collins, Jane Ireton, and Lanier Ivester who provided me with feedback on these stories.

I also thank, with a full heart, the beautiful people who have supported me on Patreon for over a year now: words cannot express my gratitude for your financial support. Special thanks to Lynne Baab, Jill Bell, Leslie Brown, June Caedmon, Rebecca Ifland, Lisa Keosababian, Amy Larson, Michelle Layton, Marilyn Roth, and Hilary Tompkins for your encouraging responses to my stories: you have no idea how much your words meant to me or how much courage they gave me to keep putting my work out there for you to read.

A thousand thank yous to Sandy Cooper and Mary K. Tiller, delightful co-hosts of the Writing Off Social podcast and fearless leaders of the Writing Off Social course, whose encouragement, generosity, and guidance gave me the courage to publish these stories and the wherewithal to publicize them without social media. Thanks, too, to the talented women in my W. O. S. cohort, who walked alongside me as I prepared to launch this book into the world: Jody Collins, Jane Curry Weber, Cara Dyck, Regina Sanchez, and Shelly Snead.

# Acknowledgements

I am indebted to Lancia Smith, founding editor and publisher of *Cultivating*, who previously published two of these stories and one of the sonnets and whose encouragement over the past eight years has been invaluable.

I am also indebted to the inimitable Wendell Berry, whom I nevertheless attempted to imitate. His "A Jonquil for Mary Penn" is the model for my "Primroses for Nell Parker." The story is largely his; the words are entirely mine. If you like my story, you will love his. Get thee to a bookstore and buy Berry's book *Fidelity: Five Stories*, in which you will find the lovely "A Jonquil for Mary Penn" (as well as four other fabulous stories).

Finally, the debt of gratitude I owe to my family cannot be expressed in words—but, being a writer, I am of course going to try! I wish particularly to thank my mother, who never wavered in her belief that I was prodigiously talented, a belief I never shared, but for which I am nonetheless deeply grateful; my father, whose estimation of my talents has always been more subdued and therefore more believable; my sister, whose courage and creativity inspire me; my husband, who for 23 years has watched me fly up on the wings of anticipation, patiently helped me back to my feet after I've fallen with a thud, and encouraged me to spread my wings yet again; my children, whose willingness to pick up the slack around the house made it possible for me to write and launch this book, and especially my daughter, who is my first and best reader and my chief cheerleader now that my mom is gone, who read all of these stories many times, and who assured me repeatedly that they were not as bad as I feared they were. I would not be where I am—or who I am—without you all.

And, of course, S.D.G. Always.

# About the Author

K. C. Ireton lives with her husband and four teenage children in the Pacific Northwest.

She is the author of two non-fiction books, *The Circle of Seasons: Meeting God in the Church Year* and *Cracking Up: A Postpartum Faith Crisis;* an ebook, *Anxious No More: 8 Habits for a Happy Life*; and hundreds of essays, articles, and blog posts.

This is her first foray into fiction.

Please visit her online at kcireton.com.

An excerpt from K. C. Ireton's forthcoming novel

# This Gladsome Light

## Chapter 1

Eleanor woke early to the sound of birdsong through her open window. Sunlight had not yet reached her room, but she could see it playing on the topmost branches of the copper beech in the yard. The purple leaves were lit as if from within. She never tired of this view from her bed, never ceased to marvel at the magnificence of this tree that she and George had planted the year they bought the house. 1932, perhaps. Or was it '33? Her memory for such details wasn't what it used to be. But she remembered digging the hole for that tree, she and George together, taking turns with their one shovel. She remembered sitting under it with her babies, a blanket spread out in the dirt because she could never get grass to grow underneath it. She remembered the day she walked into her bedroom—she'd slept upstairs then—and looked out the window and saw with wonder that the tree was taller than the house.

A breeze stirred the leaves, causing the light to shift. Eleanor lay in bed and watched the show of light and leaves and breeze, and the words of the old prayer book, which she had prayed morning by morning for decades, came to her mind without effort, and she found she was praying. The call and prayer of confession, the collect of assurance. *Grant, we beseech thee, merciful Lord, to thy faithful people pardon and peace...* She paused a moment. Something was tugging at the edge of her mind, someone who needed prayer. She waited, and in her mind's eye she saw a face she did not recognize, the face of a young man. She offered up a prayer for him, whoever he was, a prayer for pardon, a prayer for peace. The words of the Venite and the Te Deum, the Gloria Patri and the collects continued to rise in her mind, and she prayed them as they came to her, offered them up in thanksgiving for this new day of sunshine and blue sky and copper beech, of breeze and breath and the scent of coffee.

She knew Molly was in the kitchen, making the coffee, buttering the toast, and at the thought of Molly, the words of the litany circled into her thoughts. *That it may please thee to defend and provide for the fatherless children...* She gave thanks, as she did every morning, that she had woken up. She had no intention of dying anytime soon, but she felt her age and the increasing frailty of her flesh and was grateful that Molly, who had known so much loss already, did not yet have to bear the grief of her passing. It did not occur to Eleanor to consider her own loss, and when she prayed the next line about widows, she thought of Leslie and Rosemary, not of herself. *Lord, have mercy upon us. Christ, have mercy upon us. Lord, have mercy upon us.* The prayers continued to spool out, one after another, drawing her inward gaze further up, up into the canopy of the beech, up into the light shining on the purple leaves and sifting down through the branches, up into the light that was more than light, more real, more substantial, as if she could breathe it, or eat it, or bathe in it. And still the prayers unspooled silently, rising in her like the light that was rising in the sky outside, until the spool reached the end and she found herself praying the blessing. *The grace of our Lord Jesus Christ, and the love of God, and the fellowship of the Holy Ghost, be with us all evermore. Amen.*

She inhaled a long deep breath and released it slowly as she watched the light fall through the leaves for another moment. Then she rolled onto her side and pushed herself into a sitting position. Molly would be here any minute with the coffee and toast, and Eleanor wanted to be seated in her chair. Her first steps in the morning were always the most painful, and she preferred to take them alone. If Molly saw, she might insist on a walker, or worse, a wheelchair, and Eleanor refused to consider it. A cane was bad enough.

As she lowered her feet gingerly to the floor, her cat, Greyfriars, leapt off the chair where she'd been sleeping and padded softly across the room to brush her head against Eleanor's legs. Eleanor was grateful for the cat's soft, warm fur against her bare skin. She found it comforting, and this little nuzzling ritual somehow gave her courage to get to her feet each morning.

She reached for her shawl, which lay across the foot of her bed, and swept it around her shoulders. Then she scooted herself to the foot of the bed, pulled herself to her feet, using the footboard for support, and stood for a moment, bracing herself. She made her way painfully around the room, slow step by slow step, her cane in one hand and her other hand holding onto the dresser and the bookshelf, steadying herself against the wall. She hobbled the length of the room three times before she felt strong enough to let go of the dresser and the bookcase. She crossed it one last time, just using her cane, before lowering herself into her high-backed wing chair, amused and annoyed at her own exhaustion from such a small exertion.

A moment after she sat down, Greyfriars jumped into her lap and insisted on having her head scratched. Eleanor stroked her gently until Greyfriars decided she'd had enough and leapt up to the chair back and then onto the top of the bookshelf where she sat and primly cleaned herself. Eleanor picked up her brush from where it lay on the table beside her and counted 100 strokes as she pulled it through her still-long hair, which she then twisted into a knot at the back of her neck and fastened with two hairpins.

Molly could come in now. She was ready.

※

Not yet six a.m. and Tristan was already at the beach with Jess. It was completely deserted, for which he was glad. He wanted to be alone. He took off Jess's leash, found a small, thin piece of driftwood, threw it to her, and watched her chase it down the beach. A sudden stiff breeze blew in from the water, and he turned to face it, hoping it would clear his head.

He'd woken up at three and hadn't been able to get back to sleep. And he hadn't even gone to bed till almost midnight. Last night's dress rehearsal had gone badly, and Carrie had made them re-run a couple of scenes. His castmates had been game and gracious, laughing at their mistakes—well, except for Grace Crawford, whose thin smiles fooled no one.

Jess brought the stick back and dropped it at his feet. "Good girl," he said, picking it up and lobbing it as far down the beach as he could.

It wasn't the prospect of a disastrous opening night that made him wakeful at three a.m. It was the malaise that he'd been feeling the past few months. The directionless drift. As of last week, his mother was in remission. Finally. Thank God. But now he needed to decide what he was going to do. Go back to L.A. and try again? Stay here in Lindsay and get a job? Go somewhere else and get a job? What kind of job? He was only good at one thing—and apparently he wasn't good enough at it.

He shoved the bitter thought aside. After all, he was the one who'd turned something he loved into something he used, a tool that he could wield to catapult him where he wanted to land. And it had begun to work.

Until Thanksgiving last year. Or rather, the day after Thanksgiving.

Jess brought the stick back a second time and dropped it at his feet. Tristan stared down at it a moment before he bent to pick it up and throw it, his mind on that Friday morning.

"Your mother found a lump in her breast," Hal had said at breakfast.

Tristan looked up sharply. "This morning?"

"I'm sure it's nothing," Diana said.

"Last Monday," Hal said, as if she hadn't spoken.

Tristan looked at his mom. "Why didn't you tell me?"

"I didn't want you to worry. Besides, it's probably nothing."

Tristan set down his spoon, his appetite gone. "Have you told your doctor?"

Diana hesitated.

Hal said, "She saw the doctor on Thursday. They got her in for an ultrasound on Friday, and they did the biopsy Tuesday."

Tristan blinked. "That doesn't sound like nothing, Mom." He looked at his father. Hal's face was a mask, but Tristan could feel his fear. He felt his own stomach clench, but he kept his voice even. "When will you get the biopsy results?"

"Sometime next week," Hal said.

Tristan was flying back to L.A. on Sunday. "I wish you'd told me," he said. He would have flown back later in the week if he'd known, or come earlier to be with her for the biopsy.

"There's nothing you could have done," Diana said.

She was right. Still, he wished they'd told him. "You'll call me when you hear?"

"Yes," Hal said.

Diana called on Tuesday. It was cancer. "We meet with the oncologist Friday."

Tristan wanted to be there. He didn't trust Diana to tell him the whole truth. She would want to protect him. "Can I talk to Dad?" he asked. When Hal came on the phone, Tristan said, "You'll tell me everything? I want to know what's really going on."

"Yes," Hal said.

He called on Friday. Tristan could tell from the strain in his voice that it was bad. "The good news is that it's not Stage Four," Hal said. "But that's the only good news."

Three months of chemo. Surgery. Radiation.

Tristan knew they couldn't manage that on their own. Hal was still working almost full-time. And God only knew how much all of this was going to cost. It had taken him less than an hour to decide what he needed to do.

So why was it taking him so long now?

He threw the stick to Jess again.

Why couldn't he just choose a course and go for it?

But he knew why.

When he came to Lindsay last fall, he hadn't expected to be gone four months, let alone nine. He was just going to stay long enough to get his mom through chemo. But Diana had been so sick—Tristan had never seen anyone that sick in his whole life—that they'd had to delay chemo multiple times. Three months turned into four, then five. He also hadn't expected the simple fact of his absence to end so many relationships. In all these months, he hadn't heard from any of his friends in L.A., and the few people he'd called in the beginning hadn't returned his phone calls. Not his agent, not Justin, not even Genevieve. And slowly, as the months passed, his lifelong dream began to turn to dust and ashes in his mouth. He really hadn't expected that.

Jess ran back with the stick, dropping it at his feet yet again. Tristan picked it up and hurled it into the surf. He peeled off his shirt, running shoes, and socks. Then he ran after Jess. The water was cold enough to take his breath away when he plunged into it. He came up blowing hard, Jess circling him with the stick in her mouth. He took it from her and threw it along the tide line. She paddled after it, and he swam after her. The cold water forced him to focus on moving his body, on trying to keep himself warm. He and Jess swam down the beach several hundred yards before he waded ashore, shivering. The sun was still behind East Hill, and there was a cool breeze blowing in from the Sound. He ran back to where he'd left his shirt and shoes, Jess running alongside him. By the time he put on his shirt he was shaking with cold.

"Come on, Jess," he called as he ran barefoot through the sand and seaweed toward the stairs that would take him up to Park Street. At the top of the beach, he sat on a large piece of driftwood, snapped Jess's leash to her collar, and wiped the sand off his feet as best he could. Then, still shivering, he quickly pulled on his socks and shoes and set off up the stairs, taking them two at a time to get warm. He and Jess raced home. When he turned onto his parents' street, he slowed to a walk, breathing hard, but despite the cold water and the exertion of his body, his head was no clearer. He'd wasted ten years chasing an empty dream, and now here he was, finally awake from the dream, and pitifully lost without it.

❧

That afternoon, Molly sat at the kitchen table with Eleanor as they ate lunch. She wished aloud that Cecily had given her more notice and then silently chided herself. Cecily very understandably had other things on her mind, and Molly was grateful that she had remembered to call this morning, She could have waited till tomorrow morning, or even forgotten altogether and just not showed up. That would have been far worse.

Still, finding someone to usher on such short notice was difficult. "I called everyone on my list, Gran," she said. "No one's available."

She'd left two messages but doubted if either usher would be free, or would even want to—they were both scheduled for later in the run, and most people were not like Molly. They didn't want to see the same play six times, or even twice.

"Why don't you ask Leslie?" Gran said.

"Leslie doesn't want to usher," Molly said. If she had, Molly would have recruited her long before now. She could, she supposed, take Cecily's place herself, but that would mean finding someone to stay with Gran. Leslie was already coming over to be with Gran tonight, and she couldn't justify paying Meredith for a night just so she could go volunteer at the theatre.

"Perhaps not," Gran said, "but she might do it as a favor to you."

Molly knew Gran was right. Leslie was lovely like that, but it felt like a lot to ask from someone who already did so much for them. She decided to wait till she heard back from the two ushers with whom she'd left messages. Possibly this would all work itself out with no further effort on her part.

Possibly, she thought, but not likely.

❧

The phone was silent all afternoon. By the time Molly went up to dress for the theatre, she had resigned herself to asking Leslie to usher tomorrow night.

A half hour later, she stood in front of the mirror on the back of her door and surveyed her reflection. She loved this dress. She'd found it in Gran's closet, years ago, along with several other vintage dresses, but this one was her favorite, with its fitted black bodice and flared white skirt, and a short matching jacket that was perfect for Northwest summer evenings. It was too dressy for school or even church, so she only got to wear it a couple times a year. She smiled as she smoothed her hands over the skirt, glad she could wear it tonight. Then she took the jacket off—it was too warm—and tucked a black curl behind her ear, pulled it forward again, frowned at the freckles sprinkled across her nose and cheeks, blotted her lipstick, and went downstairs.

She was sitting at the kitchen table with Gran, who was finishing her dinner, when Leslie called through the screen door, "Knock knock!"

Molly waved her inside.

"Wow, Moll," Leslie said as she stepped into the kitchen, carrying a large bouquet of yellow roses and pale pink dahlias. "You look fantastic! I love that dress."

"It was Gran's," Molly said. "She wore it to Dad's high school graduation."

Leslie sat at the table and smiled at Eleanor. "You must have been the most beautiful woman there."

"You're sweet." Eleanor reached over and squeezed Leslie's hand. "But Molly looks far better in it than I did. She's got more up top to fill it out."

"Gran!" Molly sputtered.

Leslie laughed. She handed Eleanor the bouquet.

Taking it in both hands, Gran gazed at it with a look of childlike delight on her face. "Mercy, these are beautiful! Are they from your garden?"

Leslie nodded, smiling.

Molly hopped up from the table and took a gallon pickle jar down from one of the cupboards. As she began filling it with water, Leslie said, "Let me do that. You need to go." She crossed the kitchen and tried to take the jar from Molly, who shook her head and kept filling the jar.

"I have a favor to ask," she said, and added ruefully, "another one."

"Sure, what do you need?" Leslie shut off the faucet and gently took the jar from Molly's hands.

Molly watched as Leslie set the jar on the counter, took the dahlias from Eleanor, and began arranging them artfully. "One of my ushers for tomorrow night's performance got put on bed-rest this week—she's pregnant with twins—and obviously can't be there. I've called all my volunteers, and I have two I'm still waiting to hear back from, but I was wondering—if neither of them can do it, would you be willing to? You'd get a free ticket to the play. *Much Ado About Nothing*, you know."

"I do know," Leslie said, standing back to look at the bouquet, "and I already bought a ticket. Liz and I are going next weekend."

"Oh."

"Why don't you do it? You love being there." Leslie looked at Molly, who looked at Gran. Leslie said, "I'd be happy to hang out here again. Much happier to do that than show people to their seats. Besides, Eleanor usually goes to bed by nine, so I just sit on your sofa and read till you get home. It's no trouble. I'd be reading at home by myself. I may as well read here and be useful doing it."

Molly felt grateful, and a bit embarrassed. She wished she had just asked Meredith. She'd have had to pay her, but at least she wouldn't be imposing on Leslie. "That's really kind of you, Les, but—"

"I'm not being kind. I happen to like your grandmother." She nodded toward Eleanor and grinned. "She plays a mean game of gin rummy."

"Yes, I do," Eleanor said. She turned in her chair and smiled at Molly and Leslie. "I may be old, dears, but I'm not deaf. And I'm perfectly capable of staying home by myself for one evening."

"Gran," Molly said, "you know I can't do that."

"I know you won't," Eleanor said gently.

"No, I won't. I—can't." Molly suppressed a shudder, remembering the last time she'd left Gran home alone.

"I'm happy to hang out with you, Eleanor." Leslie carried the jar of flowers to the table. "You're one of my favorite people."

"And you're one of mine, dear," Eleanor said, smiling at Leslie. She nodded at the flowers. "They're beautiful."

Leslie smiled back, then crossed the kitchen to stand in front of Molly. "Listen, Moll," she said softly. "I want to do this for you. And you kind of need me to. So stop feeling like you have to be all capable and independent and let me help. Besides, like I said, it makes me feel useful."

Molly nodded reluctantly before smiling at her friend. "Thanks, Les. You're a gem."

"Well, I'm happy to come sparkle over here tomorrow night if you need me to. I'll wear my blouse with the sequins. Now get out of here."

Molly laughed. She turned to Eleanor and said lightly, "I'm going to head out now, Gran. I'll be back late, so I'll see you in the morning."

"Enjoy the play, dear."

"I will." Molly leaned over and kissed Gran's cheek. "And we'll go together on Sunday, okay?"

Gran patted her hand. "I look forward to it."

Molly felt relieved. She hated to be at odds with Gran, even for a moment. She turned to Leslie. "Thanks, Les," she said again.

"My pleasure. Now scoot."

Molly gathered her purse and jacket from Gran's easy chair by the back door, stepped onto the back porch, and took a deep breath of the warm evening air, inhaling the scent of the honeysuckle that covered the porch rails and posts.

As she descended the porch steps, she heard a loud whirring sound and looked up. A fuchsia-crowned hummingbird was flitting around the honeysuckle. "Well, hello," she said, stopping where she stood on the second step, and smiling. She watched the hummingbird dart from blossom to blossom, so close she could hear its wings whirring, until it flew away, and suddenly she felt happy and excited. She was wearing one of her favorite dresses to one of her favorite places to watch the opening night of one of her favorite plays. In exchange for handing out programs and showing people to their seats, she would get to see the play for free. Afterward there would be a reception and she would get to chat with her friends over champagne and hors d'oeuvres.

And she had just seen a hummingbird.

She all but skipped down the brick path to the garage.